Cage the Darlings

Elora Bishop

Cover image © Annnmei | Dreamstime.com
Cover design by Elora Bishop

For my beloved --
you make, of my life, great magic.

Acknowledgements

Without the support, confidence, belief and love of my beloved WOLF (Women of Lovely Feedback) Pack, my stories would be lifeless, sad things. Bree, Jen and Tara are the cornerstone of the life and magic of this novel. I am indebted to them deeply--I love you so, so much, ladies. Thank you, in the least zombie way possible, for your brains.

I want to thank Naomi Clark for keeping my secret and for her tireless and dauntless support (you rock werewolf socks, lady), Ally Arendt for her unwavering awesome, Madeline Claire Franklin for nurturing the Ink Maiden blood bond (that also involves copious amounts of coffee, tea and sparkle) and Laura Diemer for telling me, in no uncertain terms, that the world needed this book.

My wife deserves much more chocolate than could be consumed for her editing prowess and the way she makes my life magical. I love you, darling.

There are many more beautiful people than I have space to list who I appreciate immensely, who make my writing life (and life in general) a joy. You know who you are. I love you. Thank you for reminding me that magic exists outside of fairy tales.

Cage the Darlings

...[the timid blackbird]--she that, seen,
Will bear black poisonous berries to her nest,
Lest man should cage the darlings of her breast.

-- from "The Plea of the Midsummer Fairies" by Thomas Hood

Normally, bedding a well-to-do lady is not a dangerous occupation. But the Duchess Lucretia had just fallen asleep, and I was busily trying to undo the clasp on the string of diamonds about her neck, and if she happened to wake up at that moment, it'd be *my* neck on the line. Hence the danger.

Name's Envy, and I'm *all* vice--just, strangely, not the one I was named for. The tip of my tongue darted out of the corner of my mouth as I steadied my hands and finagled with the unyielding clasp with a delicate fingernail. Lucretia moaned in her sleep and wrapped one languorous arm about my torso. I froze, hearing my heart knock loudly against my bones, almost *certain* that its racket would wake the sleeping duchess. But, no, she continued to snore loudly, and desperation made my actions a little more frantic as I struggled with the clasp.

This would *never* do. I was the greatest thief in the land, I reminded myself, cajoling, as I felt the perspiration begin to bead upon my skin. I willed myself to calmness and--as if the Goddess Luck herself was rewarding me--or heard me--the clasp gave way.

I tucked the necklace into the pocket of my discarded coat just as the Duchess snorted a little in her sleep, waking. She blinked twice and looked me up and down, alarm crossing her face before she remembered how, exactly, we'd just spent the past few hours, and then she smiled, a wide, brilliant grin that made my heart knock again. I returned the grin, bowing, sweeping up my clothes in what I hoped was a roguish manner.

"That was lovely... Will I see you again?" she murmured, voice all cake and honey. I bent down and kissed her brow, pulling on my skirts as I did so.

Here's the thing: I'm not a bad person. I just have *vices*. Totally different, right? I sleep with the ladies of the palace, and I steal something from each one of them. My target isn't usually as noticeable or outlandish as a string of diamonds, stolen from a naked lady's neck and squirreled away. I felt the need for a challenge today. Don't want to get *rusty*.

I bent down again, pressing my lips a little longer against Lucretia's brow. She and her husband had an arrangement of sorts; she'd told me about it when my shirt was half off. She enjoyed a different girl every night. I wouldn't be missed.

And, judging by the row of gilt boxes and treasure chests along the far wall, neither would the string of diamonds.

Fully clothed, I blew her a kiss and made my dramatic exit, edging out of the bedroom door until it was shut behind me. Out and through the Duchess' living quarters, and I was in the palace proper.

Belinda--dear, faithful, out-of-her-mind Belinda--was almost knocked cold when I threw open the Duchess' door. She'd been crouched, peering through the keyhole, but was able to leap away just in time.

"Are you trying to give me away?" I hissed, helping her up. Together, we darted down the corridor, around the corner and into one of the many "secret" chambers beneath the portrait of Queen Lainia, She-Who-Decreases-The-People's-Taxes. The secret chamber was really not so secret and usually used by servants to move unseen through the palace.

For that's what we were, after all--plain, innocent, totally-beneath-your-notice servants.

"No one saw me," she retorted, holding out her hand, eyebrows raised. I cast a glance down the narrow hall, but there wasn't anyone else in the chamber. I dug the diamond chain out from beneath my left breast, handed it to her.

"Still *warm*," she breathed, touching it to her cheek almost reverently. Then she laughed, a sound like bells with a bit of bite to it. "It looks like the necklace she wore to dinner. Really, Envy, did you steal it from her neck?"

I winked at her, took my prize back, indelicately buried it beneath my bosom once more. "And what if I did? It's my greatest catch yet."

Belinda was still smiling, but it was clouded now, merriment leaking from her as she frowned. "Don't you think you might have been caught if…"

"I don't get *caught*," I said, nose upturned, tone imperious. "I mean, really, Belinda." I tugged at the cord about my neck, the charm resting at the point of my collarbones. It was heavy and warmed by my skin, a reassuring presence. The small clay creation was the shape of a sun, a symbol of Goddess Luck, and my prized possession--the only thing I had to remember dear Mother by, not that she'd want to be remembered by a charm she, herself, had stolen. She'd probably want to be remembered for her greatest heist, the one they caught her at.

Thievery kind of runs in the family.

Belinda rolled her eyes, turned away. "Whatever. When you finally get caught…"

"I don't get caught," I repeated, my litany, my truth, my prayer. Belinda shook her head, and together we walked down the corridor, shoulder to shoulder.

"When are you going to get tired of this? I hate being a maid," said Belinda, rubbing at her wrists. She sighed, stretched overhead. "I mean, it's beneath us, is what it is. We're thieves! Shouldn't we be thieving?"

"May I point out," I began, and she rolled her eyes again, sighed as I prepared for my lecture. I mean, it was a *good* lecture. It said true things. "It's autumn," I said, and jerked my thumb to the stone wall, to the beyond, which included a cold and dreary rainstorm that hadn't let up for days.

"Do you want to go back to Vice Quarters where not a *single* roof is leakless, or do you want to live out the cold months in here, like kings?"

Belinda laughed. "*Hardly* like kings. We spend all day scrubbing stone floors, and for what? So you can collect pretty baubles and carry out some *stupid* little challenge for yourself..."

"It's not *stupid*," I huffed, crossing my arms. "I *will* sleep with every lady in the castle, and I *will* steal something precious from each one, and then..."

Belinda stopped, turned to face me, hands on her hips. Her eyes were sharp, scathing, un-calm-downable. "And then what, Envy? *Then* what are you going to do? When is it going to be enough for you? When will you have proven yourself?"

I stood my ground, hands in fists at my sides...but I had no real answer for her. Her gaze softened when she saw my expression. She touched my arm, conciliatory.

"You've grown less and less careful," she whispered, leaning her head close, eyes unblinking. "What will we do if you're caught? What, exactly, are you trying to prove?"

I shrugged away from her, shaking my head. I couldn't answer her, because I didn't know myself. She was right. Of *course* she was right. Belinda was always right. I hadn't been careful lately...or, perhaps, at all. I pushed my luck each

time, each mark, almost to the breaking point. I
made every conquest more elaborate, more
impossible, and yet I still met with success.

In the dark of night, I sometimes wondered
the most ludicrous of things: was I…bored?

As if she could hear my thoughts, Belinda
snorted again, threaded her arm in mine. We
continued down the hall. "Promise me you'll be
more careful?" she said, after we'd gone a little
way. "I can't be the best friend of a dead Envy."

"Dead…" I laughed a little. "The king's *soft!*
He doesn't kill thieves. Why do you think there's
so many of them?"

"A handless Envy. A dungeoned-and-
starved Envy," said Belinda, persisting.

"You've thought of all sorts of horrid
punishments, haven't you? Such a charming girl,"
I murmured, but the joke fell flat. Belinda was
watching me with shrewd eyes.

"Promise me," she said again, insistent.

"Of course, of course," I muttered, testy.

My fingers were crossed. *Of course.*

*

It probably says something for the state of
the kingdom that thieves would rather spend a
dreary autumn and winter as maidservants than
freemen. I stripped out of my petticoats and
overcoats and too-many coats and dove into my
night shift, shivering from the cold the stone walls
radiated into the room. It had been an

unspeakably chill autumn thus far, and it would only get worse. Belinda was crazy--go back to Vice Quarters! Ha!

I tugged at my sun medallion and then scurried into my tiny bed, burrowing under my covers much like a field mouse in hay. If any of my conquests could see me now! I put my arms beneath my head and stared up at the dull, gray ceiling.

Belinda, in her room next to mine, knocked three sharp raps on the wall, our code for, "Good night! I hope you're still alive by morning." We'd practically grown up together, squabbling and quarreling and then becoming the best of friends in our hovel in the Vice Quarters, every night knocking our codes back and forth. Now I knocked once, then added two more raps. It mean, "Don't worry. I will be."

I was restless, thoughts roaming in ever-widening loops. I remembered the expression on Belinda's face, her palpable worry. Was it really that bad, taking so many risks? Was I being...*stupid*?

I needed some sort of physical reassurance. I got up silently, slipped out into the far-too-cold air of the room, and then lowered myself down to the floor, pressing my fingers against a floorboard that gradually yielded beneath them.

There was my great treasure, stored in a tiny burlap sack. Really, not that great: a few hairbrushes, some earrings, a small book, and three necklaces. The first two necklaces were gaudy things made of paste; this last one was the crowning glory. It glittered even in the dark, and I touched it gingerly, mouth twisted in a frown.

I felt…weird. Odd. Like something was missing or out of place or I'd forgotten to do a needed task entirely. I *loathed* that feeling. It crawled along the edges of my mind until it curled up within me, here to stay and positively gloating. There was something wrong, and I could feel it, but I couldn't lay my finger on what it was, and it was driving me *slightly* mad.

My instincts had kept me from death or the promise of Very Bad Things so many times in my life, I'd lost count. Thieves without instincts are dead thieves. I patted the bag back beneath the floorboard and stood, stretching, hesitant.

Oh, well, *hell*. I took up my shawl, shoved my feet into the drastically uncomfortable servant shoes and melted out of my room and into the corridor like a ghost. Maybe a really late walk through freezing cold castle passages when I had to be up at the crack of dawn was just the thing I needed!

I rolled my eyes at myself, burrowed even deeper in the shawl. *This* was stupid. But I didn't turn back.

And I didn't have to work tomorrow, after all. It was the Blackbird Feast. Rising at dawn or not, that was something to look forward to.

As I took the steps down from the servant's tower, my thoughts moved from the Blackbird Feast--my favorite day of the year--back to the dalliance of the Duchess Lucretia. She hadn't been extraordinary, had laid back on her pillow and batted false eyelashes at me, and her little fluffy dog had *watched* from his tasseled pillow, and that was just a little strange. At least I could check her off now. I blew on my fingers, let myself out into the east wing of the palace, from the tower.

Ten ladies down. Only ninety or so to go.

Perhaps that was a bit haughty of me. I wasn't certain all of the ladies could be charmed by my wily ways, perhaps weren't even attracted to the female aspect of mankind, but it didn't matter. I would do my best to sway them. Give it the old royal effort, as it were.

My feet traversed the worn paths I took on a daily basis, and finally through the kitchen and out into the gardens, beneath an embarrassment of stars. It was *so cold*, but I stood still, bathed in that light, and stared upward, transfixed with wonder. The stars were so bright tonight. So...*shiny*. My fingers itched to grasp them out of the skies, twist them about my neck like that string of diamonds I would never be able to wear, never be able to feel cold and dripping down over my skin. I stared up at the night sky, and I was surprised at the ache that echoed in my heart. This sky was too beautiful--a beauty I couldn't understand. It made me feel small.

A murmur, a soft giggle. My senses pricked as I ducked down, crouched beside the hedgerow, heart quickening as I heard two pairs of steps dancing closer. *Shit.* It was a sort of unspoken rule amongst the servants that no one was allowed outside past the brass bell's toll, and this was *well* past the brass bell's toll. I slunk lower, feeling the dig of earth into my palms, willing myself as invisible as possible.

I didn't see feet so much as skirts wherein feet probably dwelled. Two skirts, and they were close to me, but even closer to each other. They darted into view, and I heard laughter again, two voices like music, a murmur, a soft shush, and then...

I bit my lip, listening to them kiss. I didn't recognize the skirts, but that was not surprising. The upper ladies at the castle had a myriad of outfits to choose from, new ones made daily. No, but I *did* recognize one of the voices--Elizabeth, a lower duchess. They sat down on the little carved bench, and, keeping the hedgerow between myself and the pair, I was able to get a good look at them. Elizabeth and Rose. Not surprising. They'd been making moon eyes at each other for the better part of a fortnight, sighing with utmost vigor into their pudding each evening at the state dinners. This would make my self-proclaimed challenge a bit harder, if they began to see one another, but...

My thoughts were silenced when Elizabeth grasped Rose about the waist. I could see their expressions, star-brightened, and when Elizabeth leaned over Rose, when she sighed and drew her closer, something in my heart did something very strange. Something in my heart...fluttered.

"You are my greatest treasure. All of my wishes, my hopes, my dreams, they reside in you," she murmured before their lips met, before there was an ardent clasp together and not a bit of space between those two bodies. Funny, how they looked almost merged; only the color of their dresses distinguished them.

I rolled my eyes at the patent *drivel* Elizabeth had used to woo Rose. Not that it hadn't worked. But even on my worst day, I could think of lines of poetry faster than that, and certainly something less well known than "The Bard's Urging for Love," which every schoolgirl passed back and forth to each other in their primer books. I crossed my arms, smirked to myself as their murmurs turned more impassioned. When I got up to execute my escape plan--*run very quickly toward the kitchen door*--I wasn't even that stealthy about it. They didn't have the ability to hear anything but each other.

And still, at the doorway, I paused, hand on the sill, head turned back, watching them. There had been such a look of adoration on Elizabeth's face. I had never seen anything like that.

My heart tightened up, I sighed at my own stupidity, and I closed the door behind me with a resounding click.

No one but court ladies had time for poetry. Or love.

*

I woke up before Belinda came for me, already struggling into the only dress I owned, besides the one the palace made me wear. It had been my mother's dress and was--of course--a stolen object. Once, it had been bright blue, like the sky after a particularly spectacular storm, but now it was dull and gray. But it was soft, shapely around my bosom, and the ladies seemed to like me in it.

When Belinda finally came, knocking once and twice, then entering, I looked up from the edge of the bed where I was ramming on my ill-fitting slippers--not the servant's shoes, not today.

"How do I look?" I winked up at her. "Dashing?"

Belinda laughed, offered her arm. "You look completely woo-able."

The corridors down to the palace proper were abuzz with servants, all wearing the best clothes they owned, swapping thrown-away bits of lace from the seamstress rooms to dab in their cuffs, a mockery of the handkerchiefs of the nobles, but still pretty, if you didn't look too closely.

It was the Blackbird Feast day--*finally*. My favorite day of the year, and not even because no one in the kingdom was allowed to work--especially the servants.

We went down the five thousand steps in the curling spiral staircase to the servants' exit, pushing past a milling group of some of the higher maids, gossiping about the ladies. I heard "Elizabeth and Rose!" and laughed a little as we walked past. Belinda cast me a sidelong glance, but I shook my head, mouthed, "I'll tell you later."

And then we were out of the palace and devoured up by Angotha.

The city of Angotha was old and beautiful, like a stately lady--but if you were going to continue to consider her a lady, you might also admit that she was senile and a bit motheaten at the edges. Angotha had not been a prosperous city for centuries now. At least, that's what Ma said. She'd told me that, once, it had been one of the richest inland meccas in Sapphira, something I rolled my eyes at as a child, because it sounded so completely ludicrous as to seem an almost-lie. I couldn't imagine the streets teeming with rich nobles, as she told me they had, the upper houses filled with singers and artists and visiting queens and knights. Now, the crumbling roads were occupied by old spinsters who had inherited the houses and let them fall to ruin. It was not uncommon for the steeples of the older habitations to come crashing down into the streets after a particularly boisterous rainstorm.

Which, I suppose, explains the rack and ruin of Vice Quarters.

Vice Quarters existed in the oldest part of the city--the seed of the city that had begun it all. The houses crumbled, leaning against one another like drunken old men, haggard and threadbare and holey. They were filled to bursting with poor families and poor mice families and poor cockroach families. I should know. I grew up in the loudest, noisiest one--the stately, crumbling, old shack known to the Vice kids as the Envied Mansion. The name was supposed to be a joke. No one in their right mind would consider envying *anyone* who lived in Envied Mansion.

But Ma liked it--liked it enough to name me after it. Everyone knew one another in the place, took care of one another. It was like a big, raucous family far too involved in your personal business. As the years went by, Envied Mansion became fuller, and it now boasted five families on each of its three levels, but, as full-to-bursting as it was, some of the old folk of our childhoods still lived there.

So that was the first place we visited.

Mama Leone sat in the doorway, sunning herself. She was an overly tall woman that Ma had once called a giantess, but I wasn't sure if that was true or half-true or not true at all. You were never sure of anything in Vice Quarters. Mama Leone now cracked one great eyeball, then started upward, unfolding like a ladder, a great sea of scarlet skirt billowing out about her.

"Girls!" she said, and smothered us with a hug that smelled of bread and vinegar. Mama Leone was in charge of stealing most of the food for Envied Mansion, and she often put whole, fresh loaves down her shirt when the bakers weren't looking. Or perhaps they did look and pretended not to notice. When Mama Leone stole from you, your business prospered. I'd always thought she was magic when I was little, when she pulled a coin from behind my ear or threw her voice across the room. I was still convinced that she had a little magic in her, and now, after squishing all of the air out of Belinda and me, she held out a seashell, presumably taken from my mouth.

"You look beautiful, both of you. Tell me about your sweethearts," she said, grinning hugely, chin in hands. "I must know. Belinda, how is Feris?"

Belinda rolled her eyes. "Stupid as usual. I've moved on, Mama Leone."

"He had such a fetching rear," said Mama Leone, sighing. "And you, my darling Envy? Have you settled down with a lovely lady?"

"Mama, you know about my challenge," I said, winking at her. "I've settled down with so many lovely ladies!"

Her laughter roared to the heavens, and then she was ushering us in, but not before she whispered to me, "That seashell came from the city of Atalea, and it is a charm for bedding and wooing. I thought you'd might like to have it, so I *may* have nicked it for you..." I kissed her on the cheek and winked as we parted the blue curtains and were enveloped by the cacophony of Envied Mansion.

Colors, colors *everywhere*: bits of scrap cloth from the city seamstresses; ill-formed rugs from the school of weavers; and poorly dyed bits from the dyers, some stolen, some given, some thrown away to be woven together to cover every inch of the hole-filled walls, so you didn't think you were walking into a house that might fall down at any moment but a *palace* of warm and sumptuous fabrics that called out to you to stay awhile, because you were in good company.

People sat on pillows and boxes transformed into thrones by a bit of fabric. There were beds festooned in brightly colored rags, covered in children. Along the walls stood gossiping and laughing men and women, and in the center of the floor stood Andrea.

She was juggling about eight wooden balls, tossing them higher and higher into the air to the delighted cackle of the kids. Her long black mane was held back with a bit of twine. It was still incredibly odd for me to regard her as a grownup. When had this happened? When had we *grown up*?

She turned and saw us, and the juggling faltered; a ball conked her head as the others fell.

"I hate you," she muttered, rubbing her head and launching herself on us.

Andrea, Belinda, and I had been the best of friends before Ma died. But Andrea hadn't thought a foray into the palace a good idea. I recall her shouting something along the lines of, "You, Envy, are absolutely *crazy*!" So she stayed behind, continued her street performing, swallowing swords and eating fire and juggling so many things that it was a wonder her head was still intact. Now she grinned at us, slung her arms over our shoulders as the children booed--their new toy taken away.

"Why don't you have some beautiful woman challenging us to a death fight since we're making you come with us?" I asked Andrea, lip pouted. She shook her head, laughing.

"I *do* have *two* beautiful women taking me away! I'm quite lucky!"

We climbed up the stairs to the top level of Envied Mansion and then up through a tiny corridor that I had to shimmy in, and onto the roof.

Three lesser women and we might have fallen to our deaths, but we *had* grown up running around like little monsters across the easily dislodged shingles, yelling at the top of our lungs. Just like this newest generation was doing now. One of the youngest kids didn't even look like she should be crawling, let along launching herself across the roof...but I was hardly one to talk. We sat next to the crumbling chimney, looking out over the city, palace front and center, large and impossibly shiny in the early morning light.

"How goes your stupid mission?" asked Andrea companionably, fishing around in her sequined top before handing us a wrapped cookie. We took it, split it among us, licking the crumbs off our fingers.

"We're never going to get caught," I groaned. "Why are you such a stick in the mud? It's genius! More people should do it... The Vice Quarters are no place to live in the winter." I shivered, remembering.

"I can't risk that, Envy," said Andrea, giving me a hard look, joking smile gone. "And neither should you. I don't know what got in your head--"

"We're *actually* doing work there, Andrea. There's no way we could get caught." I shook my head, but Belinda looked from me to Andrea, worried.

Andrea shrugged. "I pray to Goddess Luck for you every single day. May you not lose your luck, Envy. You're stealing from royalty. You'll get caught eventually. Maybe not today, but you'll get caught." She leaned forward, eyes flickering with worry. "You're not even that good of a thief--"

"Blasphemy," I snorted, but an odd tremor of worry flared up in my belly. It's not like I hadn't worried about this before, hadn't worried about it every day since we started. But I was *right*. Winter in Vice Quarters led to death. I'd seen it too many times. I was tired of it. But I was common, and I lived in Angotha. What choice did I have?

So we were trying out royal life for awhile. I shifted, mouth set in a line, looking out toward the palace.

"Just be careful," said Andrea. "Promise me."

I crossed my fingers, and I actually felt guilty about it. I *was* going soft.

We scrambled down from the roof when the first wobbly, weak notes of a pipe drifted up to us. The children's parade was held in the noon hour in Vice Quarters, and we couldn't miss it! The little hooligans from Envied Mansion screamed and fought and were generally rolling around in tight little balls on the ground until the first notes drifted into the house. Then they leaped up, grabbing bits of cloth and sticks to beat together and make a racket with, and they trooped out and down into the street, yelling at the top of their lungs.

Andrea and Belinda and I laughed, strolling arm in arm behind them. Andrea took a few wooden balls from her satchel and began to juggle them, moving away from us. The children cheered as she danced, juggling expertly.

"She doesn't belong here..." I muttered to Belinda, who cast me a sidelong glance. "None of us belongs here, stealing to survive. I don't understand it, Belinda."

She bit her lip. "What's gotten into you?"

"Nothing," I whispered, watching Andrea dance, lithe and graceful and perfectly adept at throwing the spheres higher and higher into the air, the children whooping with delight.

A fiddle player began plucking out a tune on his battered instrument from a second-story window, and a horn player filled in the notes as he strode along behind Andrea. Soon there were drummers in the streets, beating on clay pots stretched tight with skins, and a heartbeat of music throbbed in Vice Quarters, tying every single person together. We danced, shouted, grabbed hands and whirled, Belinda and I, stomping our feet, lifting our arms to the sun. We had survived another year, with the blessing of Goddess Luck, people said--and perhaps the blessing of the Blackbird King.

That night, Mama Leone sat in the center of the first floor at Envied Mansion. We lay sprawled on the beds, shoulder to shoulder, legs entwined, comfortable and warm and full after a veritable feast of foods stolen, some plundered from garbage cans behind the palace, all good.

"Once," said Mama Leone, hands on her knees, leaning back on her cushion in the stance of the faultless storyteller, "there was a thief. He was a great thief, and a proud thief, and a kind thief. His name was Ragla, and he and his band of tricksters stole many great things. So many great things, in fact, that they had no place to put them! Why, Ragla found hiding places in trees, under rocks, in caves beneath the heads of sleeping bears. He was great, and he was clever, but he had a weakness." She held up her finger. "He wanted to prove to himself what a great and clever thief he was. So he gave himself a test: steal a treasure from the wicked Haglin, and he could retire, resting easy in the fact that he had been the greatest thief in the world."

Belinda elbowed me in the stomach, but I ignored it, eyes on Mama Leone.

"And steal a treasure he did--but not just any treasure." Mama Leone laughed easily, as she always did at this part in the story, which she'd told every year on Blackbird Feast day. "He took the Cursed Mirror from the wicked Haglin. And she caught him, hands stuck to the mirror, and she said to him, 'Ah, Ragla, you cannot have what is not yours. I curse you! Since you love shiny things so well, you must resemble that which you are. A blackbird by day, a man by night, you are cursed--leave my house!'

"Now, Ragla was a clever thief, and though he'd just been cursed, he knew how to turn it, make the best of it, as all clever thieves do." She pointed to all of the adults, eyebrow quirked, chuckling. "Why, what do you think he did? 'Curse me some more!' he told the wicked Haglin. 'I don't think that curse will do it.'

"She stared at him. 'Curse you more, you terrible man?' she roared, her fingers growing long claws, her eyes slitted like a cat's. 'Why...why...you are the most terrible thief that ever lived. The *king* of thieves!' and that was that. Ragla and his men disappeared, borne away on the winds of magic to a kingdom all their own, impossible to find by mortal eyes. And Ragla became the Blackbird King, and his merry band of blackbird thieves roamed the countryside, far and wide, stealing anything and everything--for who notices a blackbird?"

The children cheered, and we did, too, laughing. But Mama Leone held up her hand. The story wasn't done yet.

"The Blackbird Kingdom is a beautiful, magical place--but be warned. No mortal can find it. It exists in the half-world, the door standing in

Bran Wood...impossible to find. But still, the Blackbird King looks out for his children, and any theft gone right has his blessing on it. May the Blackbird King bless you all!" And there was a great roar in Envied Mansion, as we called out in one voice. "Bless us all!"

And then, quiet descended.

Belinda and I kissed Andrea goodbye, reluctantly crawling out of the rows of beds, patting our favorite kids, giving out hugs. Mama Leone said farewell in the doorway, eyes shrouded with sadness.

"You won't reconsider, Envy? Winter is such a long, hard season..." she murmured, putting a gargantuan hand on my shoulder, but I shook my head.

"We'll be fine," I told her, embracing her great bulk. She hugged me back so tightly, I thought I'd lost my breath forever.

"For the blackbirds' sakes, watch over her," she said to Belinda, then embraced her, too, and she waved us down the darkened street, lit by torches and little fires, the revelry of the Blackbird Feast seemingly just beginning.

"Can't we stay a little longer?" asked Belinda, glancing longingly at a dance that had broken out around one of the larger bonfires, fiddle music filling the air. I plucked at her arm, pulling her along.

"We want to go back into the palace with a group of servants so we're not noticed," I told her, for what seemed like the hundredth time.

"But won't all of the servants be coming in much later?"

"We don't know that, Bels," I said, tone softening. She didn't have to come with me, and we both knew it. I paused, watching the dancing around the bonfire, too. The dancers seemed so carefree in that moment, so joy filled. But winter was coming; the short days were coming, the snows, the sicknesses, the death. I rubbed at my eyes, alarmed at the sudden pricking of tears in them. Belinda looked at me, shook her head.

"Are you worried about them?"

"Nah," I said, watching the children run after the bigger kids, looping in tight circles. I was lying.

It had been my stupid idea to move into the palace. But not everyone could do such a brazen thing. Or would. And there would be so many kids this winter who--

Belinda snapped her fingers in front of my eyes. "Don't go all weird on me," she muttered, burrowing deeper in her threadbare shawl.

As we got closer to the edge of Vice Quarters, a small crowd began to grow. Not unusual on Blackbird Feast night, but they weren't...*reveling*. As we moved quietly through the crowd, I saw the nexus of the group of people, a slight woman standing close to a man, staring into his eyes so closely, their noses could have bumped. He was dressed in black, looked like a regular thief; she was far too brightly dressed to be a thief. Color drew too much attention.

"That's the Angotha magicmaker!" Belinda hissed into my ear. "I hear she's terrible." I frowned.

"What's she doing?" I whispered.

"I don't know…" Belinda began, just as the woman drew back, arms upraised, eyes wide. "You!" she said, pointing to the man, "You have a lucky future! You will find a dashingly handsome gentleman and settle down. I give you two years before you meet this lord!"

She turned around, gazing at the crowd with narrowed eyes as a few people began to chuckle. "You think I'm being funny?" she asked, drawing out the words, mocking. "You think that I cannot predict the future?"

"Oh, come on," I said, rolling my eyes, moving past the crowd, but the woman turned, pointed at me. Why *me*? Good gods.

"You! Come *here*," she intoned, but, really, I had absolutely no intention of going anywhere. Magicmakers were the worst kind of witches--the for-hire types that could do small charms and little else. The only reason she was able to hook her little claws in me was because I managed to trip spectacularly, and she caught up.

"Turn and face me!" she hissed, which I did, because I was about to bite out a scathing retort, but we ended up nose to nose, and she was actually quite pretty, and I stayed for a second, gazing in her eyes as she gazed in mine.

"You," she said, cocking her head. Her brows furrowed, and she took a step back. "You have very bad luck following you," she said, and she didn't say it in a theatrical way, a way that I could laugh at. She looked...*concerned*. My heart raced, and then I was moving through the crowd, perhaps a bit too quickly, actually shoving a few people to get away from the magicmaker, who I saw, with a glance over my shoulder, staring after me with a saddened downturn in her mouth.

"Envy, wait!" Belinda called, but I didn't, not until I was in a small alley and out of the Vice Quarters proper. I leaned against the side of the building, trying to breathe, my heart hammering.

"What's the matter with you?" yelled Belinda when she finally caught up with me, putting out an arm to hold herself up against the building, panting. "What did she say?"

"Nothing," I said, scrubbing at my eyes. I felt a glimmer of fear begin to flare in my stomach. I couldn't hear my instincts. There was fear, and there was nothing besides. I took a great gulp of air, swallowed, tried to calm myself down. An upset thief was a dead thief--how many times had Ma told me to get my emotions under control? I'd been doing so well...

"Envy..." said Belinda, holding out a hand, but I shrugged away from her. We said nothing as we made our way back to the palace. I walked, staring at the ground and not the myriad of stars overhead, so beautiful, so shining that passersby remarked on them, staring up at the heavens.

The woman was a magicmaker. And a terrible one. Her prophecy was nothing more than a silly street performance, so that she might entice people to buy larger prophecies from her for pennies. Like any good businesswoman, she'd been giving a little bit away for free to try and get me to buy it all up.

It wasn't real. It wasn't.

Belinda slid her arm through mine, lips pursed, and we walked the rest of the way to the palace in silence.

It wasn't real.

*

When the sharp rap at my pathetic excuse of a door sounded, I groaned, almost in agony.

It could not *possibly* be time to wake up.

Belinda opened the door, anyway, ripped off my covers, pushed me out of the bed. I landed in a pathetic heap of limbs and exhaustion on the dirty floor.

"May I remind you that this was all *your* idea?" she chirped, as she did every morning.

How could I forget?

I was going to have to step up the thievery sometime soon. My plan to remain a maidservant until spring was absolutely without fault--don't get me wrong--but the reality of *being a maidservant* was not my favored way to spend a day.

First, there was the banking up of fires and the emptying of chamber pots. That second task alone made me want to forget that I was human. Then there was the helping of the cookie in the kitchen. Cookie was all right, always kept back a bit of oatmeal for my and Belinda's breakfasts (the other servants had already eaten by that point, as we were the perpetual latest), and then there was the serving of the courtiers in the dining hall.

This chore was probably my most hated. Even *worse* than the chamber pots, if you can believe it. It wouldn't have been all bad, had it not been for Lady Ann.

Lady Ann, the king's niece, the girl who'd told me to drop dead in no uncertain terms when I offered what *I'd* thought to be the sweetest flattery one morning, "You look lovely today, milady." She was in possession of the most imperious, haughty demeanor of any creature I'd ever had the great misfortune to meet. Nothing was good enough for her. Her room was too cold, her bed too hard, the food ill-flavored, the suitors pompous, her ladies-in-waiting brainless.

Remarkably, she had a *line* of abused suitors out the door. Part of it was certainly due the fact that she stood to inherit the kingdom when King Allefred finally kicked the last of his buckets...but *most* of her appeal revolved around her proud, perfect gaze and visage: she was a doll with gold curls and a generous dash of red paint at her mouth, a sweet face formed by a master.

But she wasn't a doll; she was a young woman who had been spoiled her *entire life* by ladies who told her that she was without flaw.

So, of course, she was filled with flaws.

This morning, I brought up the tureen of soup--who eats soup for breakfast? Royalty, apparently--cursing my aching back, cursing myself for the fact that I still couldn't quell the flutter in my heart when I thought of the gaze exchanged between Elizabeth and Rose.

The two trysting women were at the table this morning, seated across from each other in their customary places, batting long lashes at each other *still*. Even though said dalliance had been over a day ago, their sallow, pale faces were still unusually flushed. I set the soup tureen down between them and began to ladle out bowls of a hot liquid that had little green things floating in it.

Lady Ann sat beside her uncle, King Allefred, at the head table. I could *feel* her gaze upon me, even before I turned and made my way back to the kitchens. I was a lesser servant; I only served the lower tables, but as I turned, I saw her face, her expression, and I paused. She appeared to be calculating, and thoughtful, and she was staring…at me.

Great. I clutched the tureen to my stomach as she rose, pointed an imperious little finger.

"You!" she said. Since she was looking straight at me, I could only assume she meant yours truly. I sighed, raised an eyebrow.

"Milady?"

"How dare you serve them before us?"

I shut my mouth before I could state the obvious, that I never served the head table, but the king was already shaking his head, plucking at her elbow. "Dear, would you stop? You're making your daily scene," he muttered dryly. She would have none of it. She stepped aside, neatly evading his grasp, coming around the edge of the table.

"What do you have to say for yourself?" Her voice was high, sharp. I did my absolute best not to roll my eyes as I gave my very cool, collected response:

"Absolutely nothing."

She shut and opened her mouth as I turned and opened the door for the head table's butler, bearing his own tureen of soup and limping. He'd stubbed his toe on cookie's kettle and had been doing his best to bind it up when I'd brought *my* tureen. Oh, such splendidly bad timing.

I felt her eyes on my shoulders as I left the room, raced down to the kitchen and Belinda, who was blowing the bellows on the oven.

"You have to do the rest," I panted, peeling off my frilly apron, shoving it into her hands. She opened her mouth, but I pressed a finger to it, shook my head. "Please, do the rest," I muttered, and she narrowed her eyes, nodded.

I'd been noticed by royalty. This broke *the* cardinal rule of our little who-could-possibly-notice-two-extra-maidservants-who-were-actually-thieves game. Oh, *shit*.

I plucked up Belinda's dirty apron and tied it on quickly. I could only hope that I was beneath Lady Ann's memory. Surely I was. I gathered up the small broom and pail and dustpan, beginning the rounds Belinda would have carried out, tidying lady and gentleman's rooms to the end of the servants' quarters.

These past few days had been warnings; I knew that now. I knocked and opened Lord Riley's room, began to sweep up around the fire. The Goddess Luck was telling me to lay low, stop being so foolish, stop drawing attention and--for the love of the *gods*--stop being so cocky about things.

As I worked at Lord Riley's fireplace grate, there was a shift of fabric behind me, something that made me still, hairs raising on my arms. I'd been too deep in thought, unmindful of my surroundings. Stupid, stupid Envy. This was all almost..*bad luck*.

I turned and took in the splash of sunshine from the floor-length windows in the corridor through the open bedroom door. In the doorway stood a woman bathed in light, gown gargantuan and bright, and as I stared at her, my eyes widened.

Lady Ann.

She'd followed me. She must have. She was looking at me now with an expression I couldn't quite read. It may have been a trick of the light, outlining her like a cherubim, shrouding her face in shadow. She cocked her head, angled a hand toward me, and then a finger, crooked back.

"Come here," she whispered, and a shiver moved through me from top to toe. I did as she asked, carefully looking down at the floor, at the embroidery along her hem. Shit. *Shit.*

"How may I help you, Lady Ann?" I asked, mouth dry.

She said nothing to my apology but took one step backward, and then two. "Come here," she said again, words haughty, high, but soft. I followed her as she took another step, and then another, and I realized we were headed toward her bedroom three doors down, gated by a big oaken door carved over with ivy leaves and tiny, adoring rabbits.

"Lady Ann..." I began, but she shook her head, put her finger to her lips, glanced up and down the hallway. But there was no one. Again, she angled her finger; a few more steps, and we were within her bedroom.

She moved around me and shut the door.

This was...odd.

She leaned against the door, back to it, hands at the curve above her hips, head still cocked, gaze expectant. "Well?" she asked, and I shook my head.

"I'm sorry, I don't..."

"Oh, really, you don't," she mimicked my tone and darted forward, causing me to leap like a startled animal. She grabbed my hand, drew me close, pressed it to her breast.

Oh.

"Lady Ann..." I said, voice high, too, but for all the wrong reasons. "Really..."

"Don't be modest," she practically purred, leaning against my shaking palm. "The way that you looked at me in the dining hall, all that fire. You *oozed*. I've heard the stories the ladies are telling. They say you're the absolute best."

"Best?" I squeaked, backing up a little, removing my freezing hand from the warmth of the satin at her chest. What was I *doing*? Envy, wake *up*! The next-in-line to the throne is *throwing* herself at you, doesn't *actually* want to torture you, and you're having *reservations*?

But a chill was racing through me, and every instinct I had bellowed, together and in concert: *get out now.*

"I'm sorry," I said, mind racing as I backed up a bit further. "I'm not feeling well this morning. Hence, my--um--outburst..."

Lady Ann's brow was furrowing, and several emotions welled up in her eyes. She settled on the one least hoped for but all too familiar: anger.

"Are you refusing me?" she whispered, voice low and dangerous. I paled, shook my head quickly.

"Get out," she said, and I swallowed, made up my mind in an instant, dashing toward the door. I was only too happy to comply with her request. It was only when I was past it, out in the chill hallway that the realization of what I'd done washed over me, even colder. What--*the hell*--had I been thinking?

I stood, for one of the first times in my entire life, afraid.

Oh, deities, star saints... I rubbed at my face with my hands and steeled myself. This was *not* good. I could only imagine the many-and-varied daily tortures Lady Ann could devise for me as a maidservant of the house, the maidservant who had angered her. I turned, looked up at the door, all of the thousands of carved bunnies gazing at me with sympathetic eyes. In the shadowed morning light, they appeared more scary than adorable.

Hesitantly, I knocked.

"Go away!" she shouted, just on the other side of the door. So. She'd been waiting for me to come back. I pressed my lips together.

"Lady Ann..." I tried, voice cracking. I cleared my throat, tried again. "Lady Ann, you must forgive me. I'm..." I rolled my eyes, attempted to sound a bit more sincere, "I'm feeling much better. If the lady would like..."

The door was open before I could get out my last word. Lady Ann wasn't looking at me, was actually looking past me, nose upraised, regal, haughty, but as I took her in, a few things began to click together. She...*wanted* me. She wanted this. She'd been thinking about it, planning it. Huh.

That should have done absolute wonders for my ego. But it...didn't, actually. Instead, I surveyed this lady, this *girl*, who had never had a moment of hardship in her life, had been handed everything from her first golden rattle to this, now, the threshold of a kingdom's rule. And in the moment of her gaze settling on mine, there was something there before she closed herself off to me.

Loneliness.

Oh, for Goddess Luck's *sake*. Me and my bleeding heart. I stepped forward, looked down at her, tried on my best roguish expression, hamming it up as much as was humanly possible.

"My lady," I whispered, voice low, lingering. "Forgive me…"

Her breathing intensified, and there was longing in that gaze, too. She was, what, seventeen? Eighteen? When she looked up at me, there was an innocence in her gaze, something so totally unexpected that it floored me for a heartbeat. It was replaced quickly--she was not innocent in fake expressions, coy glances--but I had seen into her, just then, and what I saw plucked at all the strings of my heart. As she drew me into the bedroom, as she stood, hesitant, waiting for me to make the first move, I felt pity for the little creature. Sympathy.

I kissed her, and I was gentle, but her soft mouth was hungry, and as she pressed against me, my skin pinpricked with pleasure, a shiver moving through me as I felt her warmth, tasted her perfumed skin, put my fingers hesitantly against the curve of her back. This was Lady Ann, I reminded myself, a litany of thought that cut through the pleasant sensations that began to drown out all logic and instinct. This was *Lady Ann*, and I needed to be careful…

But I wasn't careful. I wasn't careful when I laid her down upon the satin coverlet, when I moved over her, mouth a quest for her sighs, her murmurs, fingers carefully undoing buttons and stays and bows to get to her silken skin, and I wasn't careful when I explored every secret she possessed, every inch of her perfection, when I saw her eyes and her mouth open and how she moved over the bed and toward me and upon me.

It surprised me, how much I wanted her in that moment. I forgot my careful mores, my list of rules in conquests, because she was not a conquest when her lips found the hollow at my throat: she was liquid light, soft hair dripping like molten gold along my ribs, curious about every inch of me as I trembled beneath her.

I closed my eyes and surrendered.

Later, I watched her sleep, watched her eyelids flutter, watched her mouth open and close as she murmured something unintelligible. She was so young in sleep that it shattered me, and I didn't know why. I sighed, frustrated at my sudden weaknesses, gathered my clothes and began to put them back on, methodical.

She was the eleventh. She was the one I would remember.

As I slipped my feet into my shoes, I paused. I hadn't decided on a treasure. This was bad. You had to know what you were going to take, going in, or you'd waver on the decision, and a thief had no time to deliberate. I glanced back at the lady--still fast asleep--and raked the room with my eyes, a fluttering in my belly.

It was the first thing I saw, and I knew I had to take it. On her dresser, beside the hairbrush and mirror, beside the disheveled pile of hair combs and picks, was an equally tangled knot of necklaces. And between the piles glittered a tiny vial of perfume. I saw countless vials lined along her wardrobe, all similar enough that none would be missed. These were a favored gift from Lady Ann's suitors. She had hundreds, perhaps thousands. It was a perfect mark.

I moved forward, silent, and paused before the dresser, hands lingering over the fine things there. I picked up the vial, tucked it down my shirt to the favored hiding spot beneath my left breast, and then I let out a long, low sigh and turned.

Lady Ann was sitting up in bed. Her mouth was round and open in astonishment as she rose, clutching a blanket to her chest. She was weeping, and before she could stumble to the side of her bed, pull the cord, I knew she had seen what I'd done, was calling on the guards, knew even as I fell on my knees to beg her mercy that I would not get it.

She'd seen me steal.

Shit. *Shit.* How could I have been so stupid?

"How could you?" she wept, looking so young, so small, a *child*. "You just wanted me for my things," she said, crumpling on the edge of the bed, and in that singular moment, I felt gutted. I watched the girl weep and rise slowly, stiffly, even as I heard the guards dashing along the hallway toward the room, ever close and on call for the royalty. I knew it, then, could see it in her stance, in the way her shoulders wracked with sobs, how everyone in the world wanted something from the Lady Ann, and for the first time there had been someone who maybe didn't...and though *I* had made no promise, those moments had, for her. All along, I had only been using her.

It hadn't been like that. Not this time. Not with her. But there was not a single explanation that I could offer as the doors opened, as the guards paused in the door frame, taking in the scene of the weeping girl who would someday rule the kingdom, naked, and the thief who looked as guilty as the first sin.

"She stole from me," said Lady Ann, over and over and over again, as they took me from her chamber, closed the door, dragged me down the hall.

She stole from me.

*

For three days, I waited for my sentencing. They were the longest three days of my life, dragging from one rain-soaked hour to the next in varying degrees of gray and black, because apparently the sun had made a pact with autumn to never shine again. I tugged at my sun medallion, paced the confines of the rundown dungeon cell I now called home, raking dirty fingers through my hair, in turns beating myself up for my own stupidity and sitting in gloomy silence as I played over the moment her face crumpled with the knowledge of ultimate betrayal.

Shit.

Shit.

I had never felt guilty for *anything*. Guilt was a terrible trait in a thief who made her living by *stealing from other people*. Ma had taught me that early on, and, really--I wasn't a *terrible* person. I stole little things, things that wouldn't be missed. I stole from rich people who wouldn't notice. I never took something precious or needed. *I wasn't a bad person.*

I...wasn't a bad person? I tugged at my hair, pressed my forehead against the cold, stone wall.

Why did I feel guilty? I went through waves of that, too. I *wasn't* guilty; she was a spoiled princess. She had never known what it was like to watch your mother give birth to a little baby boy and watch him die from the cold, die because Ma was too weak to steal food, and I was too little to get away with it yet. I tugged at my hair harder, closed my eyes tight against the grim despair of the dungeon cell. Lady Ann had known none of my pain. What was her pain, compared to my own?

And, in the dark of that moment, I opened my eyes, felt my heart crack, slowly and terribly. I saw her face, again and again, how it crumpled. I wondered if I was her first time. It had seemed like it.

Gods. I *was* a terrible person. Perhaps the most terrible.

Three days of this cycle. Again. And again. And again.

It was my own private version of hell.

Where was Belinda? Was she all right? Did Mama Leone know? Did they all know, everyone in Envied Mansion, talking to each other in hushed tones that Envy was taken in, done for? I rubbed at my eyes so hard sometimes that I saw red when I opened them. I breathed in and out and tried not to worry about Belinda and everyone else. And failed.

On the third morning, the door was opened. They hadn't fed me. There wasn't a budget for the kingdom's dungeons since they were never really *used*. I was just lucky enough to be one of the few to experience the place firsthand. I couldn't even *remember* the last time King Allefred had put someone down here.

I thought I might be taken up to the throne room, sentenced by the king himself, or at least by his Minister of Affairs of the Kingdom (a title that Belinda and I always snorted about), but no. The captain of the guards, a man by the name of Rennigad, stood at the doorway to the castle proper, face drawn.

"Envy," he said, drawing out the word, voice heavy, "we searched your room. We discovered your other stolen goods. Do you have anything to say in your defense?"

His expression made me go cold, the way he wouldn't look at me, how bleak his voice sounded. I remembered how flippant I'd been to Belinda. The king was soft! He never killed thieves! But there was a first time for everything, wasn't there?

I was caught red-handed. It would be pathetic and pointless to declare the stolen things hadn't been taken by me. My heart twisted, worry for Belinda coming to the forefront. Where was she? Is that why she hadn't come? Had they found out Belinda was a thief, too? I didn't dare ask, licked my lips, searched his face for some shred of compassion. There was none.

"I have nothing to say," I said, then. It was the truth.

He sighed. I was glad, in that moment, that guards held my arms, for I felt weak, wondered if I'd fall in a swoon. I pulled myself together, anger beginning to burn in my heart. I was many things, perhaps, but I wasn't a *baby*. Envy, really, have a *shred* of dignity. I stood, chin up, waited.

"You are a convicted thief. Among other things." There was so much weight on that sentence that I cringed. What else had Lady Ann said I'd done? I remembered her back, how tiny she'd looked when they dragged me from her room, how broken. I bit my tongue, my lip, continued to stand, though I trembled. I was *convicted*. Convicted. It was such a sharp word.

"You committed an egregious crime against *Lady* Ann--she's next in line to inherit the throne…"

He trailed off, brow creased. "She refuses to leave her rooms, refuses food, weeps and wails. The king is enraged. So, therefore, you are sentenced to Bran Tower," he said, getting out all of the words in a rush. "You will be taken there now." He turned his back as shock moved through me, and then a sheer, rising panic dissolved the dignity I'd tried so hard to maintain.

"Please, sir," I said, voice high, quavering. "Please...please, sir!" But he'd turned an edge of the corridor and was gone from me.

"Please..." I whispered to the guards who held me, who looked straight ahead and would not even deign to gaze at me. My heart beat so quickly I wondered if it was a bird, if it would shatter through my bones and out of my chest to fly free.

We walked through the castle and out one of the side entrances. I saw no one and nothing, did not see the walls pass, or the rug beneath my feet, or the steps. I saw nothing as they took me through the streets of the city, as we walked through Vice Quarters. We actually took the road that led right past Envied Mansion, but there was no one in the windows, no one in the doorway. I would have given anything for a sympathetic glance from Mama Leone. But perhaps it was better this way. If I had seen her, I would have wept.

We left the buildings behind us as the forest swallowed us down with pine teeth and an oaken tongue.

We walked for half a day, and I saw *nothing*. I begged, and I pleaded, and finally I fell silent, everything within me as heavy as stone.

Bran Tower. It was a nightmare, wasn't it? A story my mother used to frighten me with as a child, a story she told me to make me behave. The tower scraped against the side of the sun, it was so tall. It let you in, door open and inviting, but it locked behind you, was impossible to escape from, kept its inhabitants until they died. I remembered the stories, stories as common as tales of the Blackbird King, as the speaking moths, as the night girls. Children's stories, surely not *true* stories.

Surely not real.

Surely.

It had been morning when I was sentenced, and now the shadows dragged long and lean along the forest floor, creating paths to trees that curled gnarled branches toward us, inviting. I shivered. The guards had moved with purpose all day, had not stopped to rest, but they did now, glanced from one to another and then ahead.

I made my eyes focus.

And I saw it.

From further back, I had mistaken it for a particularly tall tree, but as we drew closer, I could see the width of it, as wide as any of the castle towers. But, oh--so much taller. In my mind's eye, I had imagined it clearly when I was small, had carried the vision with me into adulthood. I had thought it might be about as tall as the city gates; they were the tallest things my childhood self had ever seen, and they'd always been imposing to me. Now I wanted to laugh. The city gates were a joke.

It *towered*, tall and unrelenting, to pierce the sky. I couldn't see the roof, no matter how hard I leaned back my head, could only see the interminable stones going up and into eternity. As we drew closer to the monstrous thing, I held back, I quailed, forcing the guards to grip me tighter, practically dragging me into the forest clearing that possessed Bran Tower.

In the back of my mind, singing along with the pulse, the crescendo of words impaled me, sharp, keening: *I'm going to die. I'm going to die. I'm going to die.*

There was a doorway in the side of the tower, an impressive, splintered thing that stood as tall as three guards, stacked one on top of the other. As we drew closer now, it shuddered and began to open. There was no one there on the other side, within the tower, when the tower door drew itself toward us, finally open entirely, hinges extended out like jaws.

"Go," said one of the guards, pushing me forward toward the door. I dug in my heels, pushing back.

"No, no," I said, voice hoarse from my litany of pleas, but they pushed me forward again, and I stumbled, once, twice, my palms forward to catch me…

Falling against the first step into the tower.

I turned, eyes wide as the door shuddered and, just as the guard who'd shoved me opened his mouth to say something, the door was back where it had been, as quickly as a jaw snapping shut. I hadn't seen it move, hadn't seen it swing inwards. Where there was the afternoon, the trees, the guards, the waning rays of sunshine, now there was absolute blackness.

There was not a scrap of light along the edge of the door. I heard no sound here, in the darkness, and my heart thundered against my ribs. It was over. Somehow, it was over before I'd even realized it had begun.

I was devoured by Bran Tower.

I had to get up; I couldn't sit here. I had to get *up*, and I did, one hand along the cold slickness of stone. I stumbled forward, hitting my toes against the side of a step, and there was a flare of light. The torches along the inward curve of the tower began to spark to life, guttering and shining in the pallid darkness.

I was afraid--gods, I was *terrified*--but there was not a single part of myself that could have stayed at the doorway, hoping somehow that they'd changed their minds. They couldn't, and...I didn't think the tower worked like that, the way that it had opened its door to me, ready and waiting, just like in the stories. Well, I supposed that part was true, then. It opened its door to greet and eat you up, and it would never open its door for you again.

I climbed. The steps went on forever. My panic was used up by the time I got to three hundred-something. I'd decided to start counting within sight of the door and hadn't stopped, but now I did stop to sit on a step, put my head in my hands.

All of the panic came back, my skin prickling with a feeling I couldn't overcome, of being watched. There was no one there. There couldn't possibly have been anyone there, but I had to wonder about the hundreds of people this tower had supposedly housed. Were there ghosts?

And, really, since when had I begun believing in ghosts?

That was a little better, that sideways smirk that managed to rise up out of the roiling depths of my heart to paste itself on my lips. It calmed me, soothed me, a moment of sheer eye rolling-ness at myself. I'd never believed in ghosts, in spooks, in bump-in-the-night type creatures, and I certainly wasn't going to start now.

I took two more rests, losing count of the steps somewhere between the first rest and the second. I began to believe that this was all I had ever done in my life, that my being a maidservant, that Belinda, my mother, all of my thieveries had been waking dreams. Audacity alone drove me forward after the second rest, because I had begun to needle anger in my heart, had stoked up my stubbornness, much like a fire. I refused to just *lie* there, feeling the cold of the stone seep into my body. I kept going.

Around the corner, I began to see *light*. Not torchlight but *real* light, the light of a setting sun, bright and burning and golden, and I found a burst of strength in me, because I half-stumbled, half-raced up the remaining steps…and out and into the top of the tower.

I stopped, panting, hand against the wall. It was huge, this room, with a vaulted ceiling that rose up into the peak of the tower's roof itself. In the rafters, birds fluttered their wings, and a single black feather drifted down against the floorboards. There were some furnishings--a spinning wheel, with nothing to spin; a dirty bed with coverlets strewn across the floor; a table and two chairs; an open trunk. The room was almost separated in two by a narrow partition that only reached halfway across the floor, built of oak and taller than me. I edged around it, peered past, but there was nothing beyond the partition save more windows.

There were *so* many windows; almost the entire rounded cup of walls was windows. I stepped closer, feeling awe for the first time in a long while. There were some trees nearly as tall as the tower, which surprised me, and I wondered if I'd seen the tower myself, far and distant out of a palace window, and had simply assumed it was a narrow pine. I put my hand against the windowsill, took up my fingers, stared at the dust.

I glanced about the room again, shaded my eyes from the brilliance of the dying sun. There were no bones, no bodies. I even peered under the bed. The room was in disarray, but wasn't that to be expected? It bothered me, though--and I wasn't quite certain why it did--that there was no evidence that there had been prisoners here before me, left to die.

I sat down on the edge of the bed, tested it by laying gingerly back. The netting of ropes held; it wasn't broken. I looked into the trunk. It housed some extra, small blankets, and beneath them, nothing. I drew one blanket up, shook it out, wrapped it about my shoulders. I could only imagine how cold it would get here tonight.

And then I stopped, still kneeling beside the trunk. Was I actually making a plan? I breathed in and out and looked at my hands, gripping my skirt's fabric over my thighs. Why was I making a plan? What did I think would happen?

"Nothing," I whispered to the indigo sky, to the sun slipping away beyond the edge of the world. Absolutely nothing.

I stood, blank, afraid. Resigned. No one was going to come save me. I wasn't going to be *pardoned*. People banished to Bran Tower never returned.

As I cast about again, one last time, looking for any signs of previous occupants, I paused. The guards hadn't given me food, had given me no water. It was well known that the king's men didn't make forays into the forest often, and they definitely wouldn't do so to feed one girl. I'd been left here to starve, rot, and I had been given no tools to help myself.

A sick, sudden realization devoured me whole, much as the tower itself had.

Perhaps there was no sign of people here because the people had *left* here, in the only manner they could. I stood, walked woodenly to the window, peered out and down.

Perhaps, having no choice, no hope, not wanting to endure the indignity of a death by starvation, they'd simply chosen to end things themselves.

At the first heartbeat after that thought, I felt deep revulsion. I was strong; I was clever-- surely I could think of a solution to save myself. But as I watched the sun drift lower and lower, already half-eaten, I felt any shreds of hope I had left sink along with it.

Could I do it? Could I jump? If I sat with my despair, could I convince myself that throwing my body off the edge of a tower was the most courageous act I might commit? I stood, slack-jawed and *afraid*, and I realized that if I thought about it for too long, I *wouldn't* be able to do it, and probably the best thing would be to get it over with now. Before I talked myself out of it.

The sheer coldness of the thought chilled me, chilled me even more than when I moved to the open window. The birds overhead moved, whispered and cooed and cawed to one another as I looked down and over the edge of the tower, feeling the wind buffet the bits of hair that had snuck out of my bun, drying up the sheen of sweat that had dampened my skin. I had to do it *now*. I wouldn't be reduced to a sad, pathetic starveling. Better to go out brave, courageous. Yes. It was better…

I almost believed it, had almost summoned up the nerve when a flash of black darted down from the ceiling. The blackbird was smaller than the others in the rafters, but it was still large enough, imposing, and she flew toward the open window. I stepped sideways to let her pass, heart thundering, but she did not go, paused, flapping her wings mightily to stay her flight, buffeting me with the force of her wingbeats so that I had to step back from the window. She flew out and into the burnt umber sky and was gone.

I shook my head. It was only a *bird;* it couldn't hurt me. I went up to the window again, again peered down, and this time, the shadowed little creature darted up from the trees, again flying toward the open window, but from the outside. I stepped back and aside as she came in, swooping up to the rafters, cocking her head and peering down at me.

I was angry now, angry at the stupid, *stupid* bird that was too idiotic not to know when it was about to run into something. I was angry that something that small could be stopping me from my most urgent task. But, most of all, I was angry at myself that I had done this, that I had ruined things, and so royally. The only person in all of this to blame was…me. And I was stupefied with anger at myself.

I sat down, feeling the pulse of wind from outside the tower come in through the window, wrapping its cold fingers about me. I put my head against my knees, and then I *cried*, great, wracking sobs that shook my bones, that urged the sea of tears I'd held up and inside of me for so long to come crashing out, like waves in a storm. The anger turned to self-loathing, which turned to pity, and every sad, pathetic thing I could think about was thought on, and I wanted to die, in those moments, completely.

I wanted to die.

I stood up, just as the sun slipped away, descended and gone. I put one hand on the edge of the window sill, and then I climbed up and on it, and I stiffened, waiting for the sound of bird wings, and I closed my eyes and gripped my sun medallion and hoped with every bit of my being that it wouldn't hurt…

"Please no."

I opened my eyes, heart thundering. Words. Words from inside the tower.

I turned slowly, gracelessly, gripping the window's sides, balance teetering.

There was a human form, a shape, a shadow hidden by the oaken partition, but it held a hand out to me, brown as bread, slight as breath, a small hand, a young lady's hand. Then it darted back, as if bitten. But the voice said again, "Please no. Don't."

I crouched down, mouth open, and scrambled back and into the room, holding my hands over my heart. There was someone here. But how could there be? There'd been no one when I searched the room. Were there other rooms? Trapdoors? I stared at her, even as she crept further back into the shadow, head ducked.

"Hello?" I said, the word soft with wonder. "Who are you? Are you a prisoner here, too?"

A snort, and I smiled in that first half of a heartbeat, before I remembered where I was, what I'd been about to do.

"I am a prisoner of a sort," said the girl, and the words were wry, as if coming from a grinning mouth.

"I didn't know anyone was here," I said weakly, then sat down, back to the wall, to the window I'd been about to throw myself from.

"Oh, I'm no one," said the girl, quick as a thief. She shifted; I heard the floorboards creak beneath her. "I'm more of a ghost than an anyone."

"I don't believe in ghosts," I replied automatically, rewarded by a light laugh, something warm and delicious in the air between us.

"I believe in you," she said, "so will you believe in me?"

Is this what happened when one went mad? I tilted my head, ran my fingers along the top of my knee. "Who are you? What are you? I can't...really see you. How can I believe in something if I can't see it?"

She did not answer my questions but tut-tutted. "Have you no faith?"

"No," I told her. It was the truest thing I knew.

A pause. Then, "I can't show myself to you. Not yet."

"Oh, well." I put my head in my hands, pressed my fingers to my eyes. "I don't know if I'll be around in a few days. I hear a body can't live without water for long--"

"Have faith," she said, the words warm, gentle.

A thought. "Are you...like, a good fairy?" I crinkled up my nose. Again, her laughter.

"No, no fairy. Just a wisp of a creature. Not even very good."

Another thought: "Are you here to eat up my soul or some such?"

This time, it was a true giggle. "You are very distrusting of strangers."

"I should be," I sighed. "I'm a thief. And strangers should be distrusting of me."

"Oh, a thief?" There was interest, and a cadence she used on the word, like a purr. "Tell me about being a thief."

I screwed up my eyes, tried to catch a glimpse of her outline in the darkness. It was impossible. Still, I wasn't throwing myself out the window, and I wasn't afraid of her.

"I was quite good," I said, then stopped, rubbing at my eyes again. "I was sort of good." There, the truth. "My friend Belinda and I? We were both thieves in Angotha. We'd snuck inside the castle for the winter, because it's too cold in

Vice Quarters, and we thought--hey, they wouldn't mind two extra servants, and we'd get food and lodging for the winter."

"A good plan," she said, and in the darkening room, I thought I could see a movement quite like a nod. "What went awry?"

"The plan was a little…more tricksy than all that," I said, tucking the edges of my skirts about my feet. "I was…" Oh, *gods*, this was going to sound so terrible…and, really, why was I telling her any of this? "I came up with a sort of challenge. I would have a dalliance with every single lady member of the court, and steal something from each of them."

Silence. And then: "What happened?"

"Well…I mean, I *did* have dalliances with several of them…" My hands moved as quickly as my words. "But it all fell apart when I was caught by this girl. And I felt terrible about it. And I guess I still do…" I was all a-jumble, and I fell silent, entirely unsure of what to say next. "It was just a stupid game," I said to the dark. "I never meant to hurt anyone."

It was strange, how quickly the dark fell this high up. I thought the light might have gone on forever, but now it was almost too dim to see my hand before my face. There was the soft *shush* of fabric, and then the floorboards creaked as she made her way closer to me. A ghost of a sort…but were ghosts solid?

She sat down beside me, and I felt the warmth of skin against skin as she took my hand in the dark. It was such a gentle gesture--the first one made towards me in a long while--that the prick against my throat and in my eyes told me I might actually weep. Really? *Really*? I scrubbed at my eyes with the back of my other hand furiously, trying to regain some semblance of dignity.

"It has been a bad few days, I'm sure," she said. This close, her voice was soft, low, a warm growl almost, and it made me shiver. I thought it sounded lovely. "Just..."--and I heard the way the word came out, as if she was smiling--"don't go throwing yourself off the tower yet. Stay awhile."

"I don't have much of a choice, do I?" I muttered, shaking my head. "I don't know if I'll have the courage to try again."

A nod in the shadows. "Good. Have a little faith. Things might turn out, after all." There was a long pause, during which I struggled to find something else to say, but she added, so soft I had to strain to hear her, "It's good to have someone to talk to."

"Are you really a ghost?" The question swung between us, like a star.

"Sleep now," she said. "Things will be different in the morning."

I didn't believe her. But I felt no prickle of fear, no worry. I followed my instincts, closed my eyes.

Unbelievably, somehow, I slept.

*

My throat was dry and ragged from lack of water, from sleeping beneath an open window all night. I hadn't drunk water (save for a few foul sips in the dungeon) or eaten food in four days, and everything seemed strange and light, as if I weighed nothing at all. I sat up, put my hands flat on the floor, palms against the wood.

I felt *terrible*.

A simple glance at the room, fully lit by the risen sun, confirmed what I had known before I even opened my eyes: my companion from the evening was gone. There weren't even any birds in the rafters anymore, the sun having lured them outside. A few bird droppings on my skirts were an indication to the path they'd taken. I stared at them muzzily, sighed.

My eyes lighted on the one difference in the room, and I stopped, put my hand against my heart. There was a small mug, made of bark, ludicrous, like a little sculpture, and there was an apple and some cheese, and half a loaf of *bread* on the little table beside the bed. I was obviously seeing things. *Obviously*, I had finally gone mad. I scrubbed at my eyes, blinked three times, and looked again.

No...everything was still there.

I stumbled to the bed, sat down, sniffed the air. The warmth of the yeast, the crisp scent of the apple, the mellowness of the cheese... It was all *real*. I put out my hand, and as delicately as I'd ever touched a woman, I caressed the edge of the cheese.

It was *real*.

I devoured it all too quickly, greedily drinking down the water, every last drop. I saved nothing; I did not think of the moment after that one. I devoured and--filled to capacity--leaned back on the veritable softness of the bed after the hardness of the floor all night, and I stared up at the faraway ceiling, thoughts circling my heart like clouds. My stomach protested, growling and cramping, but I placed a hand on it distractedly.

Had my…friend…from the evening brought these things? Where was she now? Perhaps down below, on the steps? I didn't think so, but I got up, anyway, rolling out of bed, over to the door. I tried it. It was locked from the outside.

I could not get back to the staircase.

I believed it to be the tower itself, not the girl, who had locked me up here. And, really, I hadn't lost anything in those thousands of stairs. I leaned against the door, turned back and took in my new, tiny kingdom.

There was a bucket behind the trunk which I used (and took some delight in tossing the contents out the window), and then there was nothing to do but go over *every single inch* of the space to try and find how the girl had gotten out. Vanished, literally. No matter how I pressed on the boards, on the walls, poking against the ceiling precariously, balanced on a chair on a chair on a table, nothing budged. There were no secrets to the tower that yielded to my questing hands, and I had to be all right with that.

Which, of course, I wasn't.

I paced the confines of the tower. By the time the sun had sallied overhead, I had learned every knot in the wood, every whorl in the table and chairs and bed, every lump in the straw-stuffed mattress. Again and again, I traversed the tower, until I thought I would go mad--or perhaps I'd already gone mad, and this was simply madness within madness.

I stopped at that point and watched the clouds. They were almost even with me, such was my height, and they looked soft and lovely, like a dream. I saw shapes in them, watched them move, watched the birds in flight, the squirrels who dared to scurry up the trees closest to me. I had thought of trying to propel myself out of the tower to slam against a tree, much like a squirrels, bouncing from one trunk to the other, but I had neither the dexterity not the surety in myself to try something so perversely simple for the rodents.

Eventually, I curled up in a ball on the bed, and I suppose I slept, because the next time I opened my eyes, it was dark again, and there was a slight shadow along the edge of the room.

"Hello," she said companionably, as I sat up, rubbed the sleep from my eyes. "Are you feeling better?"

"Yes," I said, surprised at how true word that felt. I actually smiled. "Was it you who brought me the food?"

"In a way," she said, and I could tell she was smiling, too. She sat down on the floor, a little blob of darkness in the thoroughly darkened room. "Was it enough? Are you hungry?"

"I'm all right," I said, even as my stomach growled, loud and insistent in the stillness.

"I don't have much with me this evening. Some oatcakes. I hope it's enough." She brought them to me, handed over a warm, soft bundle of cloth. The bundle spilled open in my lap, wafting the delicious aroma of honey and oats. I devoured the cakes like a wolf, licking my fingers.

"Where do you come from?" I asked, spreading the cloth over my lap, drinking up its warmth with the palms of my hands. "What are you? Who are you?" And then, with some chagrin: "I don't even know your name!"

"Names," she said, shaking her head, "are unimportant."

"Please. I must know it."

Silence. I didn't think she'd respond, but in a small voice, she whispered, "You may call me Merle."

"Merle," I said, holding my hands over my heart. "*Thank you*."

She didn't respond, ducked her head in the shadows. "And what may I call you, thief?" *Thief* was spoken with such playfulness. I liked the way she said it.

"I'm Envy," I said, and then I chuckled a little. It had been awhile since I'd introduced myself to someone. "My mother named me after the vice. But I'm not envious."

"It's a pretty name," said the stranger, "for a pretty girl."

I laughed. "I'm sure that's what you tell all of the prisoners in pitch-black towers."

"Maybe," she laughed, too, and I marveled, not for the first time in these two evenings, at the ease with which we spoke. Like old friends, women who had known one another since…well, since the beginning.

"How did you get in here?" I asked after a little while. I couldn't still my curiosity, which roiled beneath the surface of my skin, a living creature.

"I cannot tell you," she said in a single breath. Again, more silence, and I wondered if I'd said something to offend her, but she continued, "You are very courageous. To trust me."

"You stopped me from throwing myself from the window. You were kind. You brought me food…" I said, trailing off.

"But I have not shown you what I look like. I have told you nothing about me."

I shook my head. Then: "You told me your name."

A short laugh, like a bark. "Precious little, a name. A syllable. It has no weight, Envy."

"It has weight with me." I didn't understand, made to rise and come toward her, but she drew back until she was at the edge of the wall and floor and window.

"You should sleep," she said quickly, and I was about to open my mouth, tell her I wasn't tired, until I very suddenly *was*, and I lay back on the bed and slept.

*

Magic. I rubbed at my eyes, stared out at the misty morning. Of course this mysterious stranger knew magic, was able to use it. And a sleep spell was not so strong or terrible that only a high magician could wield its powers. Any street magicmaker knew how to cast them, and well. But still. It unsettled me. I had never seen anyone but the court magician use a spell; I thought of it as something high and lofty, not a pursuit of the common folk. And I was terribly common.

Again, when I woke, it was morning, and the bark mug was filled with cold water. There was an apple on the table, and fresh bread and cheese, but now a cluster of grapes adorned the edges of the simple wooden plate. I stared at them for a very long time before my stomach got the better of me, and I began to eat my breakfast. Had she conjured this with magic?

A girl who suddenly appeared in a dark, sky-scraping tower could do magic. I felt stupid to be surprised by such a notion, but I had always... I supposed I'd always thought of magic as a mysterious thing, a dark thing that shouldn't be touched. And here was someone I didn't think of as dark...*touching* it.

But why didn't I think she was dark? Why did I think she had good intentions, that she was a good person? Because my instincts believed it. I suppose, if you'd told someone other than a thief such a thing, they would think it stupid, but thieves based their whole lives on their instincts, and I knew--without any shadow of doubt--that I could trust mine. My instincts told me Merle was good, that I should and *could* trust her. And so I did.

I put magic out of my mind.

It was the longest day of my life. By noon, I'd decided that I had probably frightened her when I'd made to rise, that maybe she'd thought I was trying to see her. I hadn't been, but still--I'd have to make a better effort to avoid alarming her. She was the only part of my day that saved me. Even the food, as warm and flavorful and lovely as it all was, sat in my gullet like a stone. The day was just too long, too interminable, and it dragged out, weary and dull and everlasting.

I watched the birds in the rafters for a bit, watched how they came in and out of the window (that I would, eventually, have to shut, because it was too cold, making the room frigid). There were pigeons and doves and blackbirds, and the way they clustered together for warmth in the mews of the tower peak filled me with comfort.

That night, at sunset, I waited, back against the wall I'd first tried to step off of, into the air. I simply blinked, and she was there against the partition, but since the sun had just dipped down below the horizon, I could finally *see* her.

She knew I could see her. She stood with her hands at her sides and looked at me, eyes unwavering.

She had short, curled, cropped black hair that messily twined about her ears, pixielike. Her nose was sharp and upturned, just a little, and her face was full and round like an apple. She wore tattered black clothes, black wristlets, a black tunic over black stockings and black shoes, and she kept tugging at the edges of her wristlets, as if they could cover even more of her skin. Her cheeks were red, rosy on her nut-brown skin, and her eyes flashed in the dying light, green as poison.

She stared at me with pride and uncertainty warring in her expression. I stood, smoothed out my skirt, aware that I must look utterly frightful, and then I paused, realizing what I was doing.

I was preening myself, much like I did before my conquests.

I stopped, stared at her, abashed. There was something in her gaze, in the curve at her hips, in the swell of her calves, the flutter of her hands. Oh, good *gods*, really?

I found her irresistible.

This was ludicrous, *mad*. She'd saved me. I'd heard of ladies falling for knights who did nothing more than spread their cloaks over a puddle. Admittedly, what Merle had done for me was much, *much* more than spreading a cloak over a puddle, but I wasn't that empty-headed, that *daft*, that I would *throw* myself at a woman, even a woman as lovely as…

No. I put my palms flat on my hips, gazed at her just as steadfastly as she looked at me.

Her eyes glittered as the light died, as the orange faded to violet to midnight blue. We said nothing, but, eventually, we sat down. Only in the darkness did she break the silence. She said, "I'm glad to have kept something so lovely from the air."

I paused, heart thundering against my bones. I couldn't see her expression, would have given anything in that moment to do so. Her voice was so soft, so kind.

And, if I wasn't mistaken, it bore an undercurrent of an old friend beneath it: wistfulness.

"You're too kind," I told her, because it was the truth, grateful that the darkness hid my blush.

"Tell me about where you come from?" she asked then, and I could hear her settling, shifting her weight against the floorboards. "I want to hear about your city."

"It's Angotha," I said, pillowing myself on the crinkly bed. "Have you ever been to Angotha?"

A sigh. "Not in a very long time."

"It's a beautiful city, a small city," I said, tilting my head. "The king is very kind, and his subjects are very poor. The whole city is poor, really, but that doesn't stop us from making merry." I closed my eyes. "Some of my fondest memories are running around on the roofs in the Vice Quarters."

"Go on," urged Merle. I could almost feel the roof tiles beneath my bare feet, the warmth of the sunshine and the whoop caught in my throat. I opened my eyes.

"My ma--she was the best thief," I said proudly, then, surprising myself. "She was fast and nimble as a cat. No one ever caught her, 'til the last time." I put my chin in my hands. "She came up with the craziest schemes, and they always went true. The others, they said that Goddess Luck favored her especially. You'd have to believe it. She stole all manner of things! Once, she got away with a goose tucked under the edges of her skirts in the marketplace."

I remembered that morning like it was yesterday, the peals of laughter in Envied Mansion when Ma sauntered in, bold as you please, lifting up her skirts with a goose waddling out as if it was all perfectly usual.

Merle laughed, surprising both of us, I think, the rich cadence ringing between us like silver. "Your mother was much like you?"

I laughed, too. "There's some of her in me, it's true," I agreed. "But I'm not nearly the thief my ma was. She stole every meal she ever ate, every bit of clothing she possessed, the bowls that graced our table…everything. Me? I can hardly steal a bit of perfume without getting caught." I sighed. "I used to think I was a good thief, but it turns out--I was wrong. I'm only average. And average ones never last long." I waved about the room, to Bran Tower itself, my mouth forming into a still, small line. "As we can see."

Merle considered this. "Is that what you wanted to be, a thief?"

I opened my mouth and shut it, shocked. No one had ever asked me such a question. Had anyone asked me if I'd wanted brown curls, or to be born in Vice Quarters? There were some things you couldn't change, and what you were was one of them. I told her as much, and she considered this, too, thoughtful for a long moment.

"You don't think that you could have been anything you wanted?"

I snorted, shook my head. "I'm common," I told her, spreading my hands in my lap. "I was born in Envied Mansion--the poorest, most crowded house in Vice Quarters. I have enough charm to turn the heads of ladies, but it's common charm. I have to use my cleverness, my wits. I'm good at telling stories and usually at getting out of trouble. That's all I have."

"I think you have more than wits alone, Envy," said Merle gently. "You could do so much more than be a thief, if you desired it."

I pushed my fingers through my hair, sighed, struggling with the arguments that died on my lips. She didn't understand. No one could understood, unless they were born common like me. I shook my head. "I don't have much choice now…do I?"

We sat in silence for awhile after that.

"I wonder what Belinda's doing," I murmured, staring up and out through the windows at the myriad of stars, spread like a glowing blanket over the heavens. "I hope she's all right." I tugged at my hair a little, bit my lip.

"Belinda?"

"My friend at the castle. I told you about her…" I trailed off. I couldn't see Merle's expression in the dark, but her tone had gone cold.

"Oh, yes." The warmth came back. "She was a thief, too?"

"A petty thief. She stole little. She didn't have the delusions of grandeur I possessed," I chuckled. "She was very good to me. My best friend."

"I'm sure she's all right," said Merle, shifting to her other knee.

I hoped so, so *very* much, that by sheer hoping, perhaps I could make it true.

*

I wasn't afraid anymore, I realized that next day. I was awake when the sun rose, and I watched it come up and over the edge of the world, orange and brilliant and precious, and I felt my bones settle against the bedframe.

The trick was not thinking about anything but that very moment, the one where I cupped my hands before me and the light trickled in them, pooling over my fingers like water. I watched the way the light highlighted the already burning trees, so lovely and bright in their autumn gowns, how the light sliced through the leaves so that they almost seemed illuminated, like pages in a holy book. I watched the sunrise with a sense of astonishment. I had never before noticed how beautiful it was when it rounded the edge of the world, when it spread its light like a harvest table upon the ground. It was beautiful in a way I had never grasped before, a type of beauty I had never recognized.

I watched the sun rise, and I was at peace.

I slept. I was tired, and it was one of those good sorts of sleeps. I'd sat up all night and talked with Merle. I remembered, as I pillowed my head in my arms, my arms on my bedraggled little pillow, that, though I had told her several stories about me...she had said nothing about herself.

I was abashed. But it wasn't from lack of *trying*. She was the hardest lock to pick in the kingdom.

I had time.

When I woke, the sun had already arched well past overhead and was beginning its stately march down from the zenith to the horizon. I rubbed the sleep from my eyes, sat up and devoured my little feast--water and bread and cheese and an apple and grapes and a *pear*, oh-most-glorious-of-fruits.

I sighed after eating, stretched. Just a few more hours until sunset.

For she came only at sunset. I knew that now, had pieced it together by the second evening.

She came at sunset like magic, probably borne *by* magic.

So I waited.

I opened the windows throughout the day to let my birds in and out. I considered them *my* birds now, though they were as free as the sun or sky, would let me know when they wanted in or out by pecking rapidly at the windows they wanted open. They didn't do it often, and, really, what else did I have to do? I opened and the shut the windows a number of times, watching their graceful sweep out and down to the great evergreens, or the tucking in of their wings as they latched their claws onto the sill, landing and staying for a moment to taste one last breeze before retiring to their far-up perch.

When all of my birds had come home, when the sun finally set, there she was.

She regarded me quietly, great green eyes unblinking. "Hello, Envy," she said, words soft, like a growl or a purr or some sound between the two. "Did you pass the day well?" she asked, mouth upturned in the dying light to a smile I could not look at. I glanced back, over my shoulder and out the window at the sky that turned every shade of purple.

"I did, thank you. It's just that I am so *very* bored," I told her, groaning. "I sleep, and then there are hours to pass, and…well, I'm used to doing many things," I confessed to her. "All of this idleness does not suit me."

She considered this, cast about the darkening room. "There is the spindle," she said, inclining her head toward it.

"I'm not a spinner." I shook my head a bit too quickly. "And, anyway, I have nothing to spin." I cursed myself after I said that. I didn't really *want* to spin, thanks ever so much.

"There's the book beneath the bed," she said, words coming from a smiling mouth.

I gaped at her in astonishment, then dove off the bed and under it. She was right. There *was* a book. But there hadn't been one there when I checked...

"Magic," she whispered, as I drew it up and out, pressing my fingers over the old, tooled leather cover. I laughed a little, fingers touching the title.

"*Fair Folk Stories*," I chuckled, holding the book to my heart. "Did you put that there?"

She shrugged, tugged at her wristlets. "I couldn't say."

The book was heavy, familiar for all its smallness. I had one just like it as a child.

"Thank you," I whispered to the air, the blossoming stars, Merle. She nodded her "you're welcome."

"Ma used to read me these all the time when I was little--stories were so important in Envied Mansion," I said, reverently opening the little book. It fell open to one of my favorite stories, "The Little Wolf Girl."

"This is precious to me," I told Merle. "How could you have known?"

She shrugged, smiled. "Magic," she repeated, words as soft as feathers.

"There's a story in here," I said, paging through, "of a little robber girl. And one of a fairy mouse! And one of a kingdom of cats! And one of a blackbird girl! Oh, such stories…"

Merle seemed to stiffen, but she relaxed when I looked up, when I cocked my head quizzically. "Are they magic stories?" she asked then, nodding her head to the book.

I smiled, hugged it to my chest. "I suppose they all are. They have magic in them, each one. I'd never thought about it…"

"You know…magic is what makes your food appear," she said, hesitantly. "I know a little magic. I can teach you, if you like. It may while away the time, make you…less bored?"

I stared at her, uncomprehending for a full heartbeat, then shook my head, book dropped to my lap. "Oh, no." I shook my head harder. "No. I couldn't."

Merle shook her head. "I don't understand--"

I laughed. "I can't do magic!"

"Oh, anyone can do magic," she smiled again. "It's like any learned thing. It doesn't take impressive talent or skill. Really, it's like learning how to make a cake."

I set the book on the bed beside me, ran my finger over the binding. "Well, I don't know how to make a cake."

"Why are you so stubborn?" she asked. "Why don't you want to learn? It could help you. Over time, if you learned it well enough, perhaps it could even help you escape."

Escape. The word roared through my head. I caught my breath, stared down at my lap, at my hands, at the book.

"There's nothing...there's nothing frightening about it. Really, it's mostly parlor tricks, I promise," said Merle. She spread her hands, ducked her head, too. "But...just think about it. You don't have to decide tonight."

"All right," I whispered, and then I was the one relaxing.

"Are you...afraid of magic?" she asked, and I shook my head.

"Not...really. I just... I'm common, Merle. Common people don't do magic."

"Where did you get that idea?" she breathed. I shook my head. I didn't know. Maybe Ma told me once. It just made sense, and I told her as much.

"Everyone where I come from does magic," she said, shaking her head. "It's as normal as breathing. It's not...common or uncommon. It's just a part of life."

I traced the binding over and over, worrying at a small tear in one of the pages' corners.

I told the truth to the darkness. "I don't think I'd be very good at it."

"Oh," she sighed, and then she took my hand again, her warm one covering mine, so soft, so gentle. I stared down at the shadow of our hands together, spellbound. I admitted it to myself, in that moment: when she touched me, I shivered. There was nothing complicated about her touch; it was only a touch. And yet...

"I think you'd be good at it," she whispered, and I knew, in that moment, how close she was, for she'd leaned forward, voice so soft that--if she had been more distant--I would have not have been able to hear it. I looked up, and my nose brushed hers. We stayed, for half a heartbeat, like this, and then I cleared my throat, looked down at our hands again.

"Perhaps I could try. If you promise not to...oh, I don't know. Laugh yourself silly," I muttered. She laughed now, but it was a chuckle of amusement.

"I swear I won't," she said, patting my hand and releasing me. The comforting weight of her palm was missed.

"Now," she said, and in the dark there was a soft flare of light between us. She held it between her hands, a tiny orb of light. She looked so lovely, I stared for a long moment before I realized what I was doing. She wasn't *beautiful;* she didn't possess a--what did the ladies at court call them?--a *swan* neck. She didn't have wide, doe eyes and a classically meek expression. But I didn't like that. I never had. When a lady batted big doe eyes at me, I usually felt a little sick to my stomach. I didn't want someone meek, too soft to do anything but lie there and *bat her big doe eyes at me*. I wanted someone who would look up through long lashes and smile at me with an openness that made me lose my stomach.

Like she did. Now.

I stared, tried not to, tried to figure out what, exactly, it was about her that made my legs weak, that made all the butterflies in my heart take off at once, fluttering and dancing.

She grinned again, holding out the orb of light to me. "This is the easiest trick," she told me, voice soothing, "a parlor trick. I think you could do this, Envy."

I snorted, laughed. "That's high magic to me. Are you sure you're not a sorceress?"

She winked, held the sphere in one hand now. "I am making this by concentrating on the point in my hand where I want the sphere to appear. My palm--I want the sphere of light to appear in my palm, and I want it to be light enough to see your loveliness by."

I sighed, breath catching. Really, I had a crush as bad as any schoolgirl's. I cleared my throat. "Flatterer," I managed, voice soft. She grinned.

"You try it," she murmured. And the light went out.

"You're funny," I told her, but she took my hands in the dark, gently twined her fingers with mine.

"All right," she murmured. "Do you feel where I'm pressing against your palm?" It was so gentle, that press, that it was almost a caress.

I breathed out, nodded, said "yes," voice small, and she smiled in the dark, said, "Good. Now, I want you to close your eyes and think about light. Think about light so much that you have to concentrate all of those light thoughts onto the point where I'm pressing into your palm. Are you thinking about light?"

I was thinking about how close she was, how good she smelled, how tightly she held my hand. But I managed to try and focus on light, too, and suddenly something flared behind my eyelids, and I opened my eyes to stare, open-mouthed, at the tiny point of light in my palm.

Making it blink out instantly.

"That was *wonderful*!" Merle breathed, and then she embraced me tightly, laughing. "Oh, Envy, that's amazing! I can't believe you got it the first time!"

I was laughing, too, peals of laughter. "I...can't believe it, either. Can I try it again?"

"Of course," she said, and then she was holding my hand again, pressing down gently in the center of my palm. "Try again. Concentrate here..."

I closed my eyes, imagined light, light, light...

And there was light. I opened my eyes, stared at it, and--this time--it remained.

"Now," she whispered, removing her hands slowly. The light stayed, burning in my palm. "What you are doing is good, but--say you wanted to keep this light going for any length of time. Because, right now, you are using your own energy to conjure it, you would get very tired very quickly. We do not want a tired Envy," she said, grinning, "so you would want to take the energy from something else. What usually happens is that a person creating magic takes it up and through the earth. The land *is* energy, is completely created from energy; everything you see is magic and energy, so taking it up and through the earth is sustainable. Not," here she tapped my palm, and the light went out, "by yourself."

She was right. I felt lightheaded and blinked, once, twice. "Huh," I muttered. "But...we're not on the ground. We're in a tower."

"You can still pull magic through the stone and wood in the tower," she said, tapping the floor. "Try it. Imagine the energy coming up through the walls from the earth. Imagine it filling your slippers, then your legs, then up and through your arm to that tiny sphere of light."

I closed my eyes and concentrated. I opened them again quickly, however, for the flare of light was so tremendous that I was almost blinded by it. There, in my palm, seemed to turn a miniature sun.

"See how much stronger it is?" Merle breathed. "My goodness...you are a very fast learner."

I laughed a little, suddenly self-conscious, and the light went out.

"So, yes," she said then, grinning. "That's magic. That wasn't so very terrible, was it?"

It wasn't. And I had done it. I stared down at my hands, spellbound.

"Thank you," I managed, whispering to her. It had not escaped me that she had, once more, taken up my hand.

*

All day, I practiced the light trick, dredging up the energy from the stones and the wood, like Merle had taught me to do. I was able to sustain it for long periods, make it grow, shrink it. I was having far too much fun, and by the time that I had taught myself how to juggle a few spheres, like Andrea might have done, it was dark.

Merle was there, then, stretching this way and that, smile making her face soft. I grinned, held out a sphere of light to her.

"I've created a monster," she said, winking. "Have you done this all day?"

"It helped to pass the time," I told her, tossing the spheres in my palms. "Look!"

Merle did, indeed, look, watching me intently. When I was done juggling, I watched her, breathless, grin wide. She smiled, too, but it was a surprised smile, one I caught unawares.

"You look so happy," she whispered. "I'd not yet seen you happy."

I didn't know what to say. How was it possible that I didn't know what to say? There was no one-liner comeback, no joke I could crack... I closed my mouth, made the light disappear in my fingers.

"Can you show me how to do something else?" I asked her. She thought about it for a moment, nodded, smile shy now.

"The light trick--it's just a trick. A little magic. Some people call them charms. The next step up is a spell. Now," she said, coming closer, holding out her hand to me. I put my hand in hers, palm down, felt her warmth. It made me weak-kneed. I looked into her eyes, saw something within them, fleeting and then gone. I looked away. She cleared her throat. "A spell must be built and then set. That's when the magic begins to work. So it takes a little longer, but the results are stronger. It has two parts--the building of the spell and the setting of it. When you set it, you ignite it, or begin it... So spells can be stored in bottles or boxes or anything, really. They can even be stored in handkerchiefs." She pointed to the handkerchief on my bedside table--the one my food appeared upon each morning.

"Is the food a spell?" I murmured. She nodded.

"It's set to recreate every morning, and so it does. That one took a little bit of doing, but it's not so difficult--just time-consuming. But we won't start you with that sort of spell." She cast about. "You don't have much light in here. We could create a spell to make the trunk light up at night." She pointed to the empty trunk. "Like it has a treasure in it," she grinned.

I cocked my head, stared at the old, wooden thing. "How do I do it?"

"Just as you would with your spheres. Imagine the trunk filled with light, drawing up the energy from the earth. When it's nice and strong, hold the image firmly in your mind, and press down on it--it's a little difficult..." she trailed off. I opened my eyes.

The trunk was glowing beautifully, as if there was a heap of gold inside, reflecting light. I bounded over, peered in. I wasn't thinking about the light anymore. I supposed that was how you set the spell. I turned to ask Merle if this was, indeed, correct, when I saw her looking at me, eyes wide, mouth open a little, soft lips parted.

"You're a *very* fast learner," she smiled. "Maybe you should be teaching me?"

"Don't be silly," I snorted, secretly *glowing*. I ran my fingers through my hair, looked everywhere but at her, still staring at me, still smiling. "Thank you," I told her then. "Thank you for teaching me."

She shook her head. "It's no trouble, really...Envy..."

I looked up at her, watched her work her jaw, close her mouth. She sat on the edge of the bed, crossing her ankles and leaning back, looking up through the window at the perfectly clear heavens. The stars were so bright, they burned the sky apart. I sat down, too, next to her, looking up. It was companionable, but she leaned a little closer, and her shoulder brushed against mine. I didn't move; I stayed. In fact, I might have leaned a little toward her, too.

"It's wonderful," I said, then, sighing, "to be able to do something...well. I've been messing up a lot lately. It's been impossible for me to do anything right."

"I doubt that," she said quietly, drawing a pattern on the floor with a booted toe.

"No, really...I was caught, wasn't I?" I sighed. "But I...I can make *light* now."

"Empowering, isn't it? Making light?" She glanced sidelong at me, mouth turned up at the corners. "It's like holding a star in your hands, a star you've conjured."

I held up my hands, imagined a star there. The sphere of light looked much like a five-pointed star now. I stared at it, transfixed. "I hadn't thought of it that way," I managed.

She cupped her own hands beneath mine, holding mine. I felt her energy move through me, and then the star ascended, rising above my hands, higher and higher. It swung and twirled in the air beneath the ceiling. As I watched, it split--first in two, then four, then eight, splitting again and again. I watched, speechless, as hundreds of stars hung in the tower...*dancing*.

"Oh..." I breathed. "*Oh.* Merle...I've never seen anything so beautiful."

She sighed, bit her lip. "I have."

I glanced at her so quickly that what was on her face remained. I saw it, saw it there before she reached across slowly, so slowly that the stars spun faster, and then she kissed me.

It was chaste and soft, lips brushing against my cheek, igniting a blush there. I glanced up at her through my lashes, saw the silly little grin come and go on her face as she leaned back, chuckled a little. "I can say now," she said, glancing up at me coyly, "that you taste like stars."

I stared at her, astonished.

"Stars?" I whispered.

She licked her lips, stared up at the created heavens. "And magic. But I thought that might be a bit over the top, so I didn't say it. Stars might be a bit too much, even."

I was laughing then, and she was, too. I stared at her, completely captivated.

"Tell me..." I whispered, holding out my hand to her. She took it. "Please tell me...tell me something about yourself. Tell me a story?"

All of her relaxation evaporated, and she sat stiff and unmoving on the bed beside me. "I can't." She shook her head. "Not yet."

"But I..."

The moment disappeared. "I can't," she said again, her words panicked. She stood, brushing off her pants, her tunic. "I have to go."

The stars winked out, the room descended into darkness, and I was alone.

*

I was angry at her. And I had *every* right to be. I had given of myself, told her my stories. I knew nothing about her, and then she disappeared off into the night, after a moment, after a *kiss*? I paced the confines of the tower's space and stared, moody and morose, out at the gray skies that did not yield me my freezing rain shower.

I was in a foul temper and did not open or shut the windows for my birds that morning, not until an entire retinue of blackbirds began to bang against the glass together, sharp beaks making an incessant *rat-a-tat-tat*. Frustrated, I threw up the sash with violence, and the glass splintered but did not break, though the crack was ugly, like a tear across silk. I touched it, mouth in a little *O* of astonishment at what I'd done, and I was rewarded with a small cut for my pains, a blossom of red against my skin. The slash of crimson was bright in the dull color of the tower, and I stared down at it for a long moment, spellbound.

That afternoon, I read a fairy tale, one I hadn't remembered, teasing out the words with longing, trying to make them last for as long as I could. It was about a little boy who lived with his mother in a ramshackle house. Every night, he turned into a wolf so that he could hunt far and wide across the countryside to bring back a dinner for his mother, as they were very poor. It ended sadly, the wolf boy mistaken for a real wolf and shot through the heart with the huntsman's arrow. I closed the book with a resounding *thud* and tossed it against the headboard. I could not stomach a sad story today.

Is this how it would always be? A girl, clothed in secrecy, my only visitor. One meal a day. A constant hope and prayer for rain to wash the wear of time from me? I was so melancholy in that space, unreachable even to myself. I forgot that I had been saved from death, forgot my earlier joy at Merle's presence. She had left so abruptly, breaking the spell she'd woven tight as a net about my form. I wanted freedom more than I could understand.

I watched the sun move over the sky and felt nothing at all.

As sunset drew near, I picked up the copy of *Fair Folk Stories*, let it fall open at random in my lap. I peered down in the dying light.

"What would I give to be human again!" cried the little blackbird girl. "Ah, my very soul cries out for it…"

"Hello," said Merle, voice soft as a hum.

I did not look up from my reading, though my back stiffened. I didn't reply, held the book a little tighter.

"I'm sorry," said Merle then, and I glanced up, eyes wide. She came forward gingerly, as if walking on broken boards, and she drifted so close that I could feel her warmth. I moved toward it, like a flower to sunshine, and I watched her kneel down beside me, put out her hand and cover my own. "I left quickly, suddenly. I'm sorry," she repeated. "I am doing my best. I hope that you can believe that I am doing my best."

"I don't understand," I told her, because I didn't. Why was there such a great mystery about her story? Who was she? There were so many questions in my head and heart; I overflowed with them. But I remained silent.

She sighed, a long, drawn-out breath that held such weight.

"Forgive me," she said, clasping my hand tightly with long fingers.

"Why…why all of this, Merle?" I asked her, tired. I knew I would not get an answer, but the way she turned from me was surprising. Her back was rigid, her shoulders slumped.

"A little while longer," she said, rubbing at her eyes. "Can you bear all this a little while longer?"

"You come in and out of the tower, Merle?"

It was a never-ending moment that stretched between us, taut as heartstrings.

"Yes," said Merle, and the word was weary. She sat, hands limp in her lap.

I didn't know I would ask it until it was out of my mouth, my basest wish: "Can you take me with you?" I breathed. She was shaking her head before I even finished.

"I do not have the powers you think I do. The tower itself is powerful," she said, put her face in her hands. "Please believe me. I would release you if I could, if I knew how. I would release you in a second. I am not what you think I am."

Pity tugged at the edges of my skirts, and I sighed. "Then what are you?"

Her word was so soft, it fell to the floor almost before I heard it. But I did hear it: "Cursed."

My ears pricked, and I sat forward slowly, so as not to startle her. "Cursed? Like...an enchantment?" I whispered, but she was shaking her head, rising quickly.

"Don't go?" I asked her. I kept my voice as quiet and neutral as I could, and it *worked;* she stopped and stood quite still.

I bit my lip, tried to think. "Tell me a story," I said impulsively. "I've told you so many of mine. I know none of yours."

She thought on this for a moment, and I wondered if I'd asked an impossible thing. But she breathed out, long and low, and looked up at me.

"I love my father," she said, words sudden. "I love him so much. He's made some mistakes, but he's a good man. I look a little like him." She tapped at her nose, her temple, pointed to her eyes. "He has a funny laugh, big and bellowing, like a bull. He used to read me stories from that book of yours. He did all of the voices. The princes always sounded very nasal and silly." She looked down at her hands.

In the span of a few heartbeats, I had learned more about my visitor than I had in days. I sat very still and waited, hoping she would continue, but she did not, and the silence dragged on until it became uncomfortable, prickly. I let out my breath in a *whoosh*.

"He sounds kind," I said, rubbing at my shoulders. "Is he?"

"Very," she replied.

More silence.

"You know," I murmured, "I'm not afraid of anything anymore. I was banished here to die; I've stared death in the face." I motioned to the window. "Nothing more terrible can happen to me, and it's been very freeing, getting to this point. I'm not afraid of anything anymore," I repeated. She looked up at me, expression carefully blank.

"What are you afraid of, Merle?" I asked then, voice gentle. She looked down at her hands, and a long moment passed before I realized that the reason her shoulders quivered was because she was weeping. Fat tears dropped down on her clasped fingers soundlessly.

She shook her head, mumbled something. I slid down beside her on the floor, put my hands over hers. She didn't move away from me.

"I'm sorry--I couldn't hear you," I whispered. "Please..."

"I'm *afraid* that you will despise me if you know what I am," she said then, words slurred and thick with tears. I blinked twice, held her hands fiercer, harder, knuckles white.

"I would never despise you," I said, words sharp. "How could you think that?"

"You have no idea what I am..." she murmured, but I didn't let her finish.

"You saved my *life*," I hissed, enunciating each word. "You have treated me kinder these past few days than I have been treated in all my years. Are you a monster, a beast, a murderer? I *don't care*. I'm a *thief*, for pity's sake. I haven't a virtue in me."

She looked up then, eyes wide and weeping. "You can't mean that."

I groaned, rolled my own eyes heavenward. "I know exactly what I mean, thanks ever so much," I managed, mouth turning up at the corners. "Now, please know, Miss Merle, that you can trust me. I'm a thief, but I am the most trustworthy of my kind." I winked.

I sat back, realizing in that moment how close I'd come to her, my face, her face...her mouth. I flushed, cursing myself as the warmth crawled up my neck to my face. Her lips were soft and grimacing, and they were lovely, as was she, while she sat there weeping, silent and piteous. I reached out, carefully brushed away her tears, tasting the salt on my fingertips.

"I'm...not a murderer," she said then, shaking her head.

"Good to know," I grinned, but she'd sat up straighter, hands curled in fists on her lap.

"I feel somehow that you are going to be the greatest thing that ever happened to me, Envy. Do you know that?" She watched me for a long moment, and I could see her eyes in the dark, the flash of them. It spellbound me, how they sparked. She reached forward and clasped my hands, and that was my undoing, I think. Her fervor and passion and gentleness merged together into something so all-encompassing that I felt devoured by it.

This is what I had: a book of fairy stories. A room thirty paces across. An empty trunk. A few blankets. A little table. A bed. Light.

As I interlaced my fingers with hers, as I looked up into those beautiful, sparking eyes, I knew that what I possessed was infinitely more than the confines of one small prison. Even one *legendary* prison.

I had her.

How was this possible? How had this happened, how had this flourished, how had this spun from the filaments of my deepest despair and the darkest moments of my life? How had this seed grown, nurtured by my tears and heartache, by the greatest mistake I had ever made?

I couldn't ask these questions, because if I did, this tender, delicate spell circling about us, born and made from heartstrings, would shatter.

And I couldn't bear that.

I shut my mouth, watched her. She tucked a stray lock of hair behind an ear then looked at me, eyes now not bright but *burning*.

"What if you knew the truth about me? Of what I am. Would you..." She broke off. "I am afraid," she said, words small. "You are precious to me."

"Precious..." I repeated the word, touched my lips with a finger, and then I reached out, soft, tentative, and touched her lips. "Why?" I asked then. It came out sharper than I had intended, but that was because hot tears burned at the edges of my eyes suddenly, begging to descend. I did not let them. "Why am I precious to you?" I asked her. Merle watched me, shook her head.

"I have waited so long for you," she whispered, words heated. She breathed out, looked down at her hands.

"You can trust me," I said then, and I reached out, placed my hand over her heart. I felt her heartbeat raging, felt her warmth, and I shuddered, closing my eyes. "You can trust me," I repeated. "Please trust me."

She took my hand, turned it over, pressed her lips to my palm, closed her eyes. She gripped my fingers so tightly I felt her heartbeat. "Envy, I am," she said, slowly, carefully, "the daughter of the Blackbird King."

I watched her, head cocked, waiting for the last part of the joke--why had she chosen this moment to joke?--but she stared at me so insistently, without a trace of humor, that I had to swallow. Was she...serious? No, she couldn't be serious...

I waited.

She dropped my hands, put her head in her palms, cried out, "I knew you wouldn't believe me! Oh, I feel so *stupid*." She bit out the words, struggled to her feet while I sat on the rough floor, speechless.

"You're serious..." I whispered, but she was backing away from me, shaking her head.

"I knew you wouldn't believe me," she repeated, and the waver in her voice broke my heart.

"Just stop," I said, putting up my hands. "Please. Just let me think." She paused, and I rubbed at my eyes, and I *tried* to think.

It was a fairy story, of course, just like Mama Leone told it. The Blackbird King was a sort of saint of thieves, had his feast day, had those who professed undying love for him, kissing carvings of blackbirds before heists...but he, and everything about him, was a *story*.

I sat very still for a long moment.

Hadn't Bran Tower been a story, too?

Merle only came at night.

The blackbirds at the window...

The blackbirds...

I looked up, stared at her, eyes narrowed: her short black hair, pointed about her ears, her helpless gaze. I watched as she clasped her hands before me, knelt down.

"Please," she whispered, "please believe me."

I cast a quick glance to the window. The night had just sunk to full darkness. No matter what transpired this evening, it would be impossible to *know* the truth until morning. I was a stranger to faith, a woman of little to *no* belief. After all, the only faith I'd ever had was in myself, and look where that had gotten me. But as I looked into her face, her earnest, pleading face, I sighed, gingerly reached out again, touched her tears with my fingers.

"I...I believe you," I said, voice a whisper. It was the truth.

She watched me. After a long moment, the tension seemed to drain out of her, and she settled a bit more companionably next to me. Our shoulders brushed as we sat back against the bed, watched the stars come out from behind banks of clouds beyond the windows. Relief drained through her body, and, gradually, she sought my hand in the half-light/half-darkness that the glowing chest provided.

"The story is true, you know," she said then. "The story of my father stealing a treasure from the Haglin. It was a hundred years ago, when the curse began. It feels good to finally say it," she finished, words trailing off in the dark.

I glanced sidelong at her, but I couldn't see much. Her nose was upturned as she stared at the heavens. I considered her outline, her long lashes that curved down to that delicate nose. She had fine features, finer than any lady at King Allefred's court, bones as fluted and delicate as a bird. Which...made sense, if she was one.

"A hundred years," was what I brought myself to say, cleared my throat when it came out hoarse.

"Yes," she said, and ducked her head. "It doesn't seem like a hundred years. I suppose that's odd to you."

I laughed a little, snorting. "Odd is relative," I managed.

This close, she smelled of pine and wood, fresh air and rotting leaves. I hungered for that, the cold winds that must have ruffled her hair-- perhaps her wings, if I was actually beginning to believe her (was I beginning to believe her?), that wide-open space of the woods, the air above the trees and the never-ending freedom of the forest. I longed to be able to walk in anything but circles, to run, legs pumping, breath fast and shallow as I raced between the trees. Free.

But, I supposed, she wasn't free, either. "Where is your father?" I asked. "Isn't he supposed to be in..."

"The Blackbird Kingdom," she finished for me, nodding. "He is. He's there."

"Then...why aren't you?"

I heard the shift of fabric as she turned to look at me in the dark. "Well," she said slowly. "Because of you."

I stayed quiet, my heart beginning to knock faster. In the dark, she reached out, brushed her fingers against my knee, found my hand.

"My father is set to…well, I suppose you can say *retire*,'" she said, tracing the curves of my knuckles with a shaking finger. "We don't… We don't *age* because of the curse, and he's just tired of it; he's tired of thieving. He's built up such a grand storeroom of treasures. He has no more needs, you see," she whispered. "He doesn't want to do it anymore. Soon, there will be no Blackbird King. But there will be a Blackbird Queen… I will inherit his kingdom."

What does one say to that?

"Congratulations" seemed a little flat, but it was what I managed, voice cracking on the word.

She laughed a little, said ruefully, "Thank you. Envy…this is very hard for me. If you can believe it, I'm trying very hard. I'm not brave like you."

I snorted. "I'm not brave," I said, shaking my head. "Magnanimously stupid--"

"No, you *are* brave. I've been taught my whole life that someday I'll take over, that I will be the Blackbird Queen." She shrugged, rubbed at her shoulders. "I don't think I'll make a very good queen. I'm too quiet, you see." She tapped her throat, looked at me. "My father--my father is very loud. Very…boisterous," she said the word wryly, mouth twisted. "I love him, but I cannot lead like he does. The people adore him. They love him so much... I'm a shadow in the background."

"The Blackbird King," I murmured, looking down at my palms. "He was always a story to me. He's this... He's a myth," I said, tasting the word. "We would say little prayers, little rhymes. We'd wish each other luck through the king--stuff like that. We even have a feast day for him. The Blackbird Feast."

She cocked her head, laughed a little. "You make him sound like a god--"

"Very much like a god." I nodded. "Not anything like a real person."

We kept our silence for a good long while. Finally, I realized what was bothering me, buzzing at the back of my head. "What does all of this have to do with me?"

"Oh," she breathed out, bit her lip. "It's...complicated."

I stared at her.

"I'll tell you... I'll tell you soon?" she grimaced, gripped my hand. "That bravery failing again. Forgive me."

"Is there anything wrong?" I whispered. She shook her head, emphatic.

"No," she said then. "Everything is *right*."

*

I knew I must have slept, for suddenly she was poking my side, sitting up, stretching, and I could see her in the early light of an almost-rising sun, anxiously watching the edge of the world where the golden orb would rise.

"It's time. Come on," she urged, pulling on my arm, dancing from foot to foot, heel to toe.

I stood, dusting off my bottom, and yawned, covering my gaping mouth with my hand. "Time for what?" I muttered, smiling at her. Then I remembered the evening. Remembered the blackbirds. I watched her carefully, mouth open. It was time for her to transform.

She stepped away from me, again looking toward the east. "I want to show you..." she whispered, combing her fingers through her hair, patting down her wristlets, the bottom of her tunic. She shook her head, closed her eyes, breathed out.

The sun came up over the rim of the world, and I stared as Merle looked up and at it. There was a shimmer of glitter, like gold and silver flashing in candlelight, and then a blackbird flapped its wings, settling companionably with little clicking claws on the floor where Merle had just stood.

I stared, mouth open. I couldn't *help* it. Merle was gone.

Well...I supposed...not really?

A blackbird stood in her place, cocking her head this way and that--beak turned up at the corners, I might have sworn. Her wings were burnished and wide, and she practically shone in the light of the rising sun as she flapped her feathers, regarding me expectantly.

"Merle?" I whispered, squatting down. The bird nodded, a quick, jerky movement, then hopped forward, waving her wings a little, almost rising off the ground.

She pecked my knee once, twice, three times, then flew to the windowsill, pecking the window three times.

...It was Merle.

Dazed, I went over and pushed up the sash carefully. The blackbird flew out and down, cawing with all of her might before taking off again.

I watched the birds wheel in lazy circles, the hawks and the doves and the pigeons. The wrens flitted from branch to branch, and among all of the feathered denizens of the sky, my blackbird girl went, wing tip to wing tip, black as night, eyes glittering, voice hoarse and shrill, piercing the brand-new light of the morning.

I began to laugh. First, it was a sharp little chuckle, but then I was laughing so hard, I couldn't stop, hand on my belly as I wheezed for breath.

Merle transformed into a blackbird girl. I was locked up in Bran Tower. The Blackbird King, kingdom and treasure were real.

All impossibilities, once upon a time.

Now, all true.

I shut the window gently, went to the bed and laid down, staring at the brightening sky with eyes that filled with laughter's tears.

I was...*happy*.

I, Envy, terrible thief, utterly common, was falling in *love*.

*

When I was small, Mama Leone was the undeniable storyteller of Envied Mansion. She sat in the center of the room, hands spread wide, eyes closed, about to begin a tale, and there wasn't a whisper from man or mouse. We loved her stories, memorized them, could probably have recited them in our sleep. But there were other ways to hear a story. Ma could read, had stolen a copy of *Fair Folk Stories* from a seller in the marketplace, and would bring it out on special nights to read to me. All of the children in Envied Mansion gathered, wrapping scraps of blankets about themselves, and they listened closely as Ma read aloud, following along the lines with her pointed finger. It almost seemed magical, as if she held on her lap a great book of spells, and she brought the magic to life by words alone.

I touched the book that Merle had given me now, picking it up, letting it fall open. I wished Ma could have seen this...all of this. I wish she could have known that, yes, maybe I ended up in Bran Tower, but I wasn't in trouble. I wasn't dead. I was falling in love, and--

I blinked, and I realized I was blinking back tears. I scrubbed at my eyes furiously, brought my fingers to my neck, touched the clay pendant there, warm like the sun, warmed by my mother's skin, once upon a time. It was my first memory of her, sitting in her lap, turning the sun to and fro in my thin little hands, amazed at how the golden paint (then, there was much more golden paint than now) shimmered in the embers of the fire.

I often berated myself for missing my mother. She was gone, and there was no bringing her back. She'd died well, had been happy when it happened, had stolen everything but the palace right out from under the king's nose, and though we were very poor and had very little, we had each other, and all the peoples of Envied Mansion and everyone in Vice Quarters. One big family, something my mother told me, over and over. The family will always take care of you. And they had.

I missed Mama Leone. I missed Andrea. I missed Belinda. I sighed, looked up at the sun, felt the sun against my fingertips.

I wanted them to know I was all right. I wanted them to know I was more than all right. But, of course, I couldn't tell them, not any of them.

I shut and opened the book again, let it fall open. Closed and open. Closed and open, the words a blur of gray. It fell, now, to a little black-and-white illustration, two girls kneeling before one another, one's face clasped in the other's gentle hands. It was a picture I had not remembered. As the sun slipped down the horizon, I read the story, read it until the sun slipped away, and I blinked in the absence of light, and she was there.

Merle stood, distant, hands deep in her pockets, half-smiling, eyes wide. "You looked so deep in thought," she whispered then. "I didn't want to disturb you."

I sighed, stretched overhead. "I was reading a story."

"What about?" She came and sat at my feet. Gently, surprisingly, she pillowed her head in my lap. I reached down, brushed my fingers against her skull, marveled at how feather-soft and thin her black locks were--how warm. I smiled, brushing my hands over the hair, tucking it behind her ear. She sighed, closed her eyes.

"The story was about a princess, of course," I told her, voice quiet in the coming darkness. "A princess and love everlasting."

"I don't remember that one," she said.

I looked down at her, at how my finger curled the little ringlets, one, two, how natural it felt, to do this.

"I can tell it to you," I found myself saying.

"Please," she whispered.

So I did.

*

Once, there was a summer child. She ran barefoot in the woods and twined wildflowers in her hair, howled at the full of the moon. She drank good cold water from the mountain stream, and she grew up to be beautiful and feral, for no one had ever touched her or spoken soothing, kind words to her. Every bit of her was wild.

She lived in the inhospitable barrens of a particular kingdom, ruled by a particular king. Now, this king knew that the barrens were inhabited by what the locals called "a wild girl," and as he had a penchant for new and unusual things, he sent his guards out into the barrens to capture the child.

She was grown up now but still innocent in all ways, and she had never spoken a word. When the guards caught up with her, she fought tooth and nail, until--subdued--she was put in a cage and the cage on a cart, and the cart went all the way to the doors of the castle before she awoke and realized what bad tidings had befallen her. Then she howled like a monster, howled like a wolf, howled like a broken creature so long and so loud that the kingdom's people flooded the streets, afraid. But there was only the girl, sad and lonely in the cage, caught.

The guards brought the cage before the king, and he was sorely disappointed. "I thought she would be a creature!" he said sadly. "Something filled with magic, a monster! But this is only a girl!"

The king's daughter watched the girl with a calculating eye, and she frowned and said, "Father, I have asked you, time and again, for a companion. May I have her?"

"She is of no use to me," said the king with a sniff, so the wild girl's cage was brought up to the princess's room, and then they were alone.

"My father is not a cruel man," she told the girl, who crouched on the edge of the cage farthest away from the princess. "He can be unkind. I don't think he means to be. I hope you can forgive him."

Of course, the wild girl said nothing.

"Are you hungry? I have so much food, any food you like," said the princess. "I can get the baker to bake you cupcakes and cookies or wild boar or pheasant or fine black bread."

Of course, the wild girl said nothing.

"Can you not speak?" asked the princess, crouching beside the cage. When the wild girl did not answer, the princess withdrew, and--if you had been there--you would have seen the tears tracing down her cheeks. For the princess had a secret. All of her life, though she had been given dolls and stuffed bears and nursemaids and jeweled crowns, none of that mattered to her. For she had been so piteously lonely that all she had ever wished for was a friend.

Now, when you are good of heart and you have been wishing a wish for so long that you know the warp and weave of it, sometimes the wish magic changes things. That evening, for example, the princess wished so hard for something good and lovely to happen that the wish became a bit of sparkling dust that the wild girl caught in her eye. She blinked ferociously; she blinked meekly. But no matter what she did, the wish was caught, until a single tear escaped, rolling down her cheek.

And just like that, the wild girl asked, "Can you please let me out? I hate cages."

The princess sat up, mouth open. "I thought you could not speak!"

"I thought so, too," said the wild girl. "Please let me out."

And the princess did.

"I thought you might bite me," she confessed to the wild girl. "I'm still not so sure that you won't."

"I won't," the wild girl promised, sitting in the middle of a rug flecked with gold, looking very out of place and strange.

"Are you hungry?" the princess breathed, and the wild girl said that she was, thanks ever so much, and the princess brought her cupcakes and cookies and wild boar and pheasant and fine black bread, because she was too excited to choose, and the wild girl ate it all, licking her fingers clean.

"Is there anything else you might like?" asked the princess.

"I would like to go home," said the wild girl.

This was not what the princess wanted to hear, not one bit. But she was a good girl, and she knew that the wild girl did not enjoy the palace, not even a little. So she went to the stables and borrowed two horses, and--in the middle of the night--the princess and the wild girl rode back to the barrens.

The barrens was a very rough place, much too rough for princesses, but she was brave and wanted-- more than anything--for her new friend to be happy. So, though the creaking forest frightened her, though the one-eyed monsters in the bog seemed to call her name, she ignored it all and urged her stallion onward, and, together, they reached the wild girl's home.

Now, the wild girl had a secret, too, and it was this: though she howled at the moon and drank from the stream and played with the mountain goats and ate wild dandelions, she had always been terribly lonely.

When they came to the wild girl's home, a very little shack in a tiny meadow beside a tall, tall pine, the wild girl hesitated and turned to the princess.

"Though it may be a tiny shack and a tiny meadow," she told her, "it is still roomy enough for two. If you'd like to live with me."

The princess fell off her horse with happiness, and--together--they made a wild home for two out of the wildest love imaginable.

And if you find a tall, tall pine guarding a tiny meadow with a very little shack, you can tell them I said so.

*

I grinned down at Merle as she straightened, eyes wide.

"Did you like it?" I asked her, smiling, but she nodded quickly, swallowed.

"I know what I must do," she whispered. "Envy...please...you must listen," she said, rising to her knees, reaching for me in the dark. I breathed out in surprise when she cupped my face with her hands, skin as soft as feathers.

"I came out into the world, Envy," she said, voice quiet and still, "because I was in search of a bride. That was my father's one wish. If I was to inherit the kingdom, he wanted to make certain that I would have someone at my side. He doesn't want me to live like him, alone. He's been so lonely..." she trailed off. "I didn't think I could do it, but I promised I would try. I spent each day as a blackbird, each night as a woman, and I've been searching; I've been everywhere, but finally I came here...on the day they brought you... And it seemed like fate. I...think it was."

She became silent, and the air hung heavy between us.

I reached up, placed my hands over hers on my face, felt how they trembled there, how she trembled before me, bravery failing. She sat back on her heels, withdrew herself from me, but I paused her, and our fingers brushed against one another in the dark.

"I am falling in love with you," she said simply.

The words lingered like music after the last note, fading away into the night. I felt so much in that single moment, emotions raging, perhaps more than I'd ever felt before, but in the roar of my heartbeat, the honest answer sought its way to the seed of who and what I was, and it came to a single truth, as still as water.

I reached out, eyes wide in the dark, and took her hand. I remembered that moment between Elizabeth and Rose, remembered my constant longing, the ache in my heart for something I believed a common woman could never *possibly* attain. Love was for royalty; love was for ladies who embroidered hearts on handkerchiefs, not for women who scrubbed at blackened pots and *completely failed* at being a thief.

Ten thousand words jostled about in my head, but I couldn't speak. I didn't dare. I held her fingers, and I pressed my lips to them, to the rise of her thumb, to her cool, sweet palm, and I breathed out, long and low, as her breathing quickened, as she said something too soft for me to hear.

But she repeated it, leaning down to my ear, lips brushing along the skin of my neck as if tasting the words. What she said was, "Thank you."

I didn't know what to do. I, Envy, the woman who decided to make a game of seducing all the ladies of an entire *castle*, was suddenly at a loss as her mouth lingered there on my neck, breath warm and soft, making me shudder.

"You've found your bravery," I murmured, sat up, still clasping her hand. Her mouth against me smiled in the dark.

"What do we do now, you and I?" she wondered aloud. "Do you...do you feel the same, Envy?"

I said one word, "yes," drew up her hands to my heart, touched them to my cheek. "Let's unwrap this slowly. Let's come to it together. I want to learn you, learn every part of you. I want to know what makes you laugh, what makes you blush..." I teased a finger over her wrist, rewarded with a shudder. "I've never had love. It was only a game before," I said, biting my lip. "I want...I want to do this right."

She nodded in the dark, and when she spoke, I heard a smile in it: "We have time, Envy."

We spoke a little more, of silly things, of stories, then curled up together, her head on my shoulder, and slept on and off until the morning.

*

That night, I very carefully began to ask my ten million questions.

"Do you sleep? Have you really lived a hundred years? Why do people think the Blackbird King is a story? What's the Haglin like? Does this mean that eventually I'll get out of this tower? Are you mortal? Can you do more magic than the little enchantments, like making me sleep? What's it like...*flying*?"

She listened, then she laughed, relaxing down onto the floorboards beside me. She didn't reply, only leaned forward, and gently--almost tentatively--she kissed me on the cheek.

"I brought you something," she murmured, shy, and handed me a bit of wildflower. It only had three purple petals, but it still smelled lovely-- the very, *very* last of the season. In the tower, winter was always on my mind...but here was a reminder that autumn still lingered.

"Thank you," I laughed a little, putting the flower behind my ear in my tangled mess of mane. "You know," I said conspiratorially, eyebrow raised, "I used to be the one to do the wooing. You'll spoil me, you know."

Merle blinked, surprised, her face softening. "Is that what I'm doing?" she asked, head cocked--very much like a bird, I realized. "Wooing?"

"Like a schoolboy with a burning heart," I said, grinning back. I took up one of her hands, turned it over, kissed the palm again. She smelled leaf green, like earth and branch. "I like it very much."

"You are so lovely," she whispered, and I looked up too quickly, saw the fervor in her eyes before she glanced away, tucking a wisp of hair behind her ear. "Forgive me," she whispered. "I...I say what I feel. It is too much...?" I shook my head.

I watched Merle, watched how she spoke, brightly now, no longer afraid. The way she moved her shoulders, cocked her head, grin wide and inviting and utterly infectious, ate me up in small bites until I realized that my heart was mushy.

We spoke long into the night, shoulder to shoulder, hands clasped, easy, as if we'd known each other much longer than a handful of days.

Toward morning, as the sky began to lighten, Merle considered the fading stars. "I have been giving much thought to Bran Tower," she said slowly. "It is an enchanted place, and it resists certain magics, but any enchantment has its weak points. Its power is to keep any soul that enters through its doors for eternity." She moved up onto her knees, cocked her head. "But no one has ever tried an audacious act...such as using a rope ladder." Slowly, saucily...the blackbird girl winked.

"Do you have a rope ladder?" I asked, grin wide. She shook her head but stayed my sadness with a raised finger.

"But I know where I can get one. Steal one..." she amended, smiling. "Tonight will be our last night together in this place, Envy... I'll fetch the ladder and a hook, and we'll get you out and down and away from here."

My heart soared at the mere *thought* of my feet on good, solid earth once more. I sighed, pressed my fingers to my collarbones, stretched a little. As Merle stood, as I followed, the sun began to rise, a sliver turning into a lick of flame on the horizon.

"Good morning," I whispered, and brushed my lips against her cheek as she closed her eyes. A flash of light made me blink, and the blackbird fluffed her feathers at my feet.

I let her out of the tower, feeling the cold lick of wind against my bare arms as I shut the window once more. I shivered, ran my fingers through my tangled mess of hair.

I spent the day sleeping and reading and wondering about things. If Merle was going to be the Blackbird Queen, that meant I'd be a queen, too. Would I have to wear fancy dresses and walk stiffly? I'd seen the ladies with the books on their heads. I wrinkled my nose, ran my fingers along the edge of the windowsill as I walked around the room again. If it was truly a kingdom of thieves, like the stories suggested, surely the people didn't dance around in fine brocades and listen to harp music. I hoped. I didn't think I'd be cut out for a life like that.

But... And here I paused, coming to the crack in the glass again, like a line on a map. I traced my finger beside the crack, careful not to touch it. I had the odd sensation that fine brocades, harp music or no...I would be perfectly happy. If Merle was there.

I rolled my eyes at myself, but I was grinning, too.

I'd gone soft through and through.

It was delicious, this falling in love. I understood now what the poets meant, what all the songs tried--so terribly--to convey with their rhyming lyrics and dulcet overtures on passions and bosoms heaving. Well. It wasn't like that. It was so much more than that. It was fire, and it was burning in my veins, and it was this *thrumming*, this rhythm that my heart prepared and sang every time I thought on her. When I thought about her smile, the way she turned her head, her gaze, the softness of her lips, the warmth of her hands...I couldn't breathe. I took in breath, but it wasn't enough, and the whole world turned light like air, and I supposed that love was an elemental thing, a wild thing, unruly and impatient and *wonderful*.

I missed her. I wanted to thread my fingers through hers, laugh again as I explained what a maidservant did (reach up *very high* to dust the statues! I'd pantomimed), and she tried to convey what it was like to catch a current with sparking wings.

And, toward the end of the afternoon, as the chariot of sun trundled down, down to darkness, I curled up on the bed and closed my eyes, and I imagined what spending the rest of my life with her would look like.

I laughed again, but only a little this time, and I was surprised to feel a wetness against my cheek, and I put up my hand and touched tears.

I had thought my life was over. I'd thought I was dead. At the lowest moment in my entire life, when I had thought--a true, clear thought--that every last bit of luck I'd ever had evaporated and was gone, it all came crashing back in one great wave.

I was falling in love with a blackbird girl, and I would be her queen.

A rapping and a tapping came at the window, and I threw myself out of bed and across the floor to open the sash as the sun slipped below the horizon, and Merle sank down from the sill into my arms.

"Hello," she said, and then she kissed me. A real kiss, a warm kiss, a soft kiss that tasted of sunshine and berries as she gathered me into her arms, and she was in mine, hands against backs and pressing, holding, as we found the perfect place, as if we'd belonged here, now, at the shattered end of day, heart to heart and mouth to mouth, as we kissed like the first kiss, I would imagine--all soft and unknowing and gentle. Gradually, this fell to carnality, for I drank her up and in, and suddenly I was hungry, starved, and when she broke away, gasping, when I did, I put my lips to her neck and her skin, and she tasted like I hadn't expected, or perhaps I had--that green sharpness on my tongue as I traced it down to her collarbones, and I was reminded of cobalt skies and unfurling leaves and the thousand tongues of trees when she laughed against me. We were weak in each other's arms with our foreheads pressed to one another, because I couldn't get closer to her than skin against skin, and I wanted to but didn't know how.

"I've waited so long to meet you," she whispered, arms circling my waist, words circling my heart. "I've waited my whole life. Forever," she said, and the word was broken and small and sad, and when I kissed her this time, the gentleness returned. I wanted to patch up that broken word on my blackbird girl's tongue, for it didn't matter anymore. Here and now we were; we were together. We were.

"I'll come for you tomorrow night," Merle promised, as we sat on the edge of the bed together. "I have my sights set on a rope ladder." She dug into a little satchel at her side and produced a hook, a curve tipped with wicked sharpness that was larger than her hand. There was a coil of rope in the bag, too, as thin as my little finger. I glanced at it nervously.

"You won't climb down on this," she assured me. "You'll let the hook grip the edge of the windowsill, with the rope attached, and drop it down to me, so that I can tie it to the rope ladder. You'll draw it up, then climb down, as easy as can be."

"As easy as can be," I repeated. I'd never been a fan of heights.

"The Blackbird Kingdom," said Merle, gesturing toward the north, "is just through Bran Wood. It's really only a few hours' walk, if that. I went home today," she said then, grinning widely. "I told Father about you. Oh, Envy, he's so excited..." She put her arms about my shoulders, held me tightly. My heart did little flips. This was really happening. The Blackbird King--the saint of thieves--was going to welcome me into his lost kingdom to be a queen.

I ran my hands through my hair. "I hardly look presentable," I said, struggling upright, out of her arms. "I'm sure I look a fright..."

"No," said Merle, a whisper. "You look...*beautiful*..."

I laughed a little, smile twisted sideways. "You are blinded by my charm, darling," I winked. "I assure you--I'm certain I look a wreck. I don't know if I want to go before a king like this."

"Well, I know a spell..." Merle gave me an apprising look. "But I don't know--"

"Oh, *please*," I breathed, dropping to my knees before her, smile wide and probably a touch creepy. "I'd like to be magicked to look slightly human again. Please? I don't want to enter the Blackbird Kingdom like a beggar."

Merle nodded. "I did it while you were still talking."

I blinked, looked down at my hands, my ragged and ratty and no-one-alive-should-be-wearing-this night shift. It was gone, replaced by a modest and charming blue cotton dress. And my hands? My hands were clean and *washed*. I reached up, touched my hair, coiled in a single braid down my back. *Clean*. I could have wept but squeaked with joy, instead, and I launched myself onto my blackbird girl.

"I must go and fetch the ladder, must make arrangements," she said, sitting up. I fell to the side and rolled out of bed.

"You're leaving?"

"I must," she said, voice low. "But I will return, and then we'll leave this place forever..." She sighed, reached out and gently, gently cupped her hand at the nape of my neck, reached up, traced the skin to my chin. I shuddered, looked up into her eyes, her green-as-poison eyes. They were filled with longing.

"I will return, and I will take you away from here," she said, "and someday you will be my queen, my bride. I will wait."

"Wait," I said, and I gripped her arms, her wrists, her hands. "You can't leave like this." There was a tear in my belly; already the emptiness of her departure gnawed at me, wicked.

"Wait…" I whispered, wishing, wanting more time.

I didn't know what would happen when we got down, when I was freed. I didn't know what the kingdom would be like, what the king would be like, what would change between us. Merle had not thought of the rope ladder idea until last night, but I wished now, strangely enough, that we hadn't thought of it for awhile longer. I was taken care of here; I was *clean* now. What else did I need? I looked up into her eyes and felt something important and precious falling away, and I did not remotely understand myself. Wasn't freedom the most important, the all-consuming truth of my life? Wasn't the good, solid earth beneath my feet more important than a little more alone time? I mean, *really*, Envy.

But as I watched her, as I felt this new thing, fragile as a baby bird, blossoming and beating wings against my heart, I knew the truth.

"I…" I began, feeling the blush spread. I--I was *blushing*. Oh, how soft I'd gone! But before I could outthink myself, before I could let my newly found shyness eat me up with velvet jaws, I put up my hand, and I placed it against the curve where her neck met her shoulder, a delicious bit of bare skin before the blackness of her tunic. I rested my fingers there and felt the heat and warmth of her, felt her shudder beneath my touch, eyes closed, lips parted.

And I kissed her. I kissed her gently, warmly, letting my fingers drift below the collar of her shirt, and she opened her eyes, and we broke away, and she was breathing hard, and I could feel the pulse beneath my palm, could feel her heart beating in every inch of me, for my own heart responded. We stared at one another, spellbound, silent.

"Don't go," I said, and I meant it, meant it to the shining moon, the orb suspended in the perfect, dark sky, and back. I lowered my gaze, looked up at her through long lashes, and then I was laughing a little as I cocked my head to the side, put my fingers up to the first button on the blue cotton dress, remembered in that motion the many, many times I had done this, how--in those moments, long ago--it had meant nothing but the pleasure of that connection, knowing full well that it would fade with the morning light.

I undid the first button; my fingers slipped as she breathed out, breath catching, staring, transfixed at my fingers. She looked at me then, and she *smiled*. Oh, gods, that smile. I stepped forward, and I was kissing her again, and I was undoing *her* buttons with deft fingers, and then she was doing mine, though clumsily, and we lay down on the bed, struggling with our respective garments, laughing until we were weak and senseless. And then I climbed on top of her, and I kissed every inch of her, and she sighed, and she whispered my name, and she held me so tightly that our heartbeats twined together, and there was no ending or beginning of skin or heart or hope or love, for they twined together, as did we, and though I'd found myself, every single time, comparing, there could be no comparison on this one, I knew. She was good, because she knew what I wanted, and I was good because I loved her, and when we moved together, we created new patterns, new languages that I had never experienced--though I'd thought I was experienced--or knew or had ever known. For this action, this ritual, was now something sacred and funny--even as we laughed when I almost fell out of the bed, ever smooth--and delicious. Oh, moon and stars, it was *delicious*.

I stared down at her from overhead, my stars to her earth, watched the way the moonshine made her eyes glow, the way her black hair shimmered in the starlight, the way she smiled up at me, arms entwined about my neck, into my hair.

"I've waited…" she whispered, but I didn't let her finish. I devoured her mouth, and she tasted of a hidden, languished hope that had seemed impossible.

That hope tasted like green and sweetness and light. And, for some completely fascinating reason, vanilla.

I knew what she was going to say, you see. I knew it, because I could have said it, could have said it in my dreams, in my darkest moments, in my most joyful.

I've waited for you.

*

Eventually, after everything, she kissed the palm of my hand, and she shimmered and was gone.

I felt a great tear of emptiness. The dark of the rest of the evening stretched out, interminable and lonely. I wrapped my arms about my frame, and then I sat down gingerly on the edge of the bed, staring out at the blanket of stars that lay suspended in the heavens.

I still tasted her on my lips, still felt her warmth against me. But she was gone.

But...*tomorrow night.*

I lay down and slept, content.

*

I actually *sang* that morning--poorly and out of tune, but I sang old nursery rhymes and drinking songs and a really bawdy rendition of "Let the Geese Out" that Ma used to sing to *me* when I was little and still learning the meaning of certain phrases. I laughed as I sang it, and I made the bed. I fluffed up the dirty blanket and the pillow, and I closed the trunk that had lain open for who knew how long. I set the room to rights, and I opened and shut the window for my birds, and--toward nightfall--I opened *all* of the windows, shivering as I sat on the edge of the bed. I wanted the birds to be able to get in and out without my help. Because they wouldn't have me anymore.

Because soon, soon I would be *gone.*

I played with the rope and hook, winding the rope around the bottom of the hook three times, removing it three times. Over and over and over again, as darkness fell. I drifted to the open windows, kept peering down below the branches, but there was no one there.

How big *was* this rope ladder? Where did she need to bring it from? As the sun set and the moon began to rise, I realized I didn't even know which direction she'd be coming from.

I walked from window to window, peering down into the dark below. It was a sedate pace I set for myself, but as the night wore on, my stomach began to tighten. Where was she?

The night was endless. The sky began to brighten, the stars winking out one by one, and I gripped a windowsill, swaying on my feet as I peered down at the damnable earth.

Merle had not come.

I didn't know what do. *I didn't know what to do.* Where was she? I knew, knew as deep as my bones and past them that she wouldn't have *not* come. She had always come. Fear licked my skin as I wavered there in the dawn, peering down, shaking. I was actually shaking. I looked at my hands, my quivering fingers, tried to smooth down the front of my dress, ran my fingers through my hair. Tried to breathe. I sat on the cold, rough boards of the floor and drew my knees up to my chest and breathed in and out.

Merle had not come.

On the edge of the bed sat the hook and the rope. The rope was so thin--so *thin*--and it was so far down to the ground. I tugged at my hair, pulled so hard that the pain blossomed along my scalp, cutting through my haze of worry, fear, cutting to the heart of the matter. I had to get down. I had the tools, albeit poor ones, to make this happen. If I could get down to the ground, I could find Merle...

But what if she had only been delayed? What if nothing was the matter? My instincts told me this wasn't the case, and I had to trust them. Merle would have come for me, no matter what, and she hadn't.

But still. What if my instincts were dulled, out of practice? I tugged at my hair again, stood, strode across the tiny tower again and again and *again*.

I don't know what I would have done if I hadn't heard a familiar voice calling from outside.

My heart leaped up into my throat, and I lunged toward the window. "Merle!" I cried joyfully, peering down at the ground...

But it wasn't Merle.

It was Belinda.

She stared up at me, far distant, hand shielding her eyes, cloak's hood fallen back. Even from this distance, she looked tattered, worn, but I would recognize that furrowed little brow anywhere.

"You're alive!" she cried, and then I realized she was crying, her shoulders shaking as she buried her face in her hands and knelt down on the earth.

"Belinda, I'm okay! I'm okay," I called out to her, waving my hand, still feeling my heart beat against my throat. I couldn't imagine her walking through the forest, couldn't imagine her entering the cursed wood--*Bran* Wood--couldn't imagine her searching for me. She hated the cold, the mud, the outdoors in general, and yet she had *come for me*. I was crying, too, then--cursing myself, even as the tears streaked down my cheeks.

"You're an idiot!" I called out, and laughed. And she was laughing, too. We stared, up and down, at one another, and I had never felt so grateful for her friendship in all my years.

"How did you find it?" I asked her, shouting the words. She shook her head, shrugged in an exaggerated fashion, shoulders rising up to her ears.

"That's not important. I'll tell you later!" she shouted back. "Why aren't you dead?"

"Thanks ever so much!" I laughed again, then sobered. I should be dead. And I would be. If it hadn't been for Merle...

"Did you see a woman in the woods? Or...I mean, a blackbird? Did you see a blackbird?"

"Have you gone mad?" she shouted up, voice cracking. "There are blackbirds everywhere! What are you talking about? Are you mad? Don't throw yourself off the tower! Get back inside!"

"I'm not mad," I hissed down at her. "It's important... I'll explain later," I added. "What do we do now?"

She shrugged. "I have a rope. But it's kind of paltry. I didn't even know if you'd be alive..." she said, shading her eyes, words trailing off to a softness I could scarcely hear. I wondered if she was crying again. I couldn't bear it if she was.

"I do, too...and a hook. But...I don't know if it can hold my weight."

Her brows furrowed again. "If you had a rope and a hook-- Wait, how did you *get* a rope and a hook? Why haven't you tried to escape?"

"It's a *really* long story, Bels," I groaned. "I'll tell you all about it later. I'll try coming down now."

I cast a glance about the room again, heart aching. Where was Merle? I took up *Fair Folk Stories*, shoved it down the front of my dress and gingerly grasped the hook. The mouth of the windowsill was too wide for it to hook properly, which would likely result in me falling to a nice and grisly death. I supposed I could hook the rope around the bed, but would it support my weight?

"What are you doing?" Belinda called up. I waved a hand at her out the window, trying to think.

I looped the rope around one bed leg, tested it uncertainly, and pushed the bed up to the window. I cast about one last time, then dropped the rope down to Belinda. It reached all the way to the bottom. Okay. I could do this.

I had no idea what to do, really. I sat down on the sill, stuck my feet out over oblivion, then felt my stomach drop away from me. I turned over, scooched back a little, holding onto the rope as tightly as I could with my hands.

I began to climb down.

I was scrappy and wiry and strong. But after three or four shiftings down, one hand after the other, my arms began to tremble so violently, I thought I might fall then and there. Squeezing with each finger and palm as tightly as I could was a nightmare I would not soon forget.

It went on forever, the climbing down. My hands' aches blossomed to bright red pain that hammered through me in nauseating waves. I risked a glance over my shoulder, then regretted this choice fervently.

"You're doing so well!" Belinda called up, though her voice wavered, and I think she was just as afraid as I was.

If I fell, I would die.

I'd wanted that once. I didn't want that anymore.

Eventually, my feet scraped against something. In the haze of pain, I felt about a bit with my toe, wondering if there was a scrap of ledge, perhaps, along the tower that I could rest against for a short, or long, moment...

But then something ran into me, and I toppled to the dirt, rope slicing out of my hands as Belinda embraced me.

I was on the ground.

The *ground.*

I sank down to my knees, and Belinda sank down with me, holding me so tightly that I couldn't breathe. I tapped her arm, taking in a great lungful of air when she relaxed her grip. She was crying. In my entire life, I had only seen Belinda cry twice: once when her father died-- caught in a heist gone wrong--and once when she broke a rib from a bad fall out of a mark's mansion.

And now...this.

"It's...okay," I whispered, patting her arm awkwardly. She sniffled, stopped, sat up and looked at me.

"I tried to reach you in the palace. I did. Oh, Envy, I thought they were going to kill you," she whispered, taking the edge of her cloak and mopping up her face. "Then it was rumored they took you to Bran Tower, and everyone thought they *had* killed you. But I went to a magicmaker, and I traded my father's ring--"

"Oh, no, Belinda, you didn't," I said, and I was almost in tears, too. I scrubbed at my eyes furiously. My sun medallion was the only thing I had to remember my mother by. Belinda's father's ring was the only thing she had from him. It was pure gold, and small, but a ruby chip in the center made it worth something. She'd worn it on a chain about her neck every day since he'd died.

And...*that* magicmaker?

"The magicmaker told me where you were, and she gave me a needle to find you." She held up a piece of string from which dangled a quivering needle, pointed decidedly at a very odd, magical angle toward me.

I stared at the needle for a long moment, rubbed my eyes again with aching, bleeding hands. I looked down to my palms, spoke a few favorite curse words, and began to rip at the hem of my dress.

"We can't go back to Angotha," said Belinda, nervously looking over her shoulder. "It all changed, after you were sentenced. Lady Ann--"

My stomach seized at that name, and I shook my head. "No. I didn't think we'd go back to Angotha."

"How are you still alive?" she asked me then, staring at me, eyes wide and...fearful. "I was so afraid..." She shook her head, couldn't finish. *I was so afraid you were dead.*

"I..." I didn't know what to say, how to explain everything that had happened to me since I'd left the gates of Angotha behind. Since I had come to Bran Tower. I cleared my throat, looked up at the massive pines that towered around us, the soft light of the sun that shone overhead. I felt the heat against my skin, my hair, my face, felt its warmth fill me. I sighed.

"There was a girl..." I began. And I told her everything.

We talked until the sun was almost slipping away, Belinda and I clasping hands like we'd done when we were little, seated knee to knee on the rich forest loam. At first, there was hearty disbelief from my best of friends. But, gradually, she looked up at the tower, crouching behind us like a terrible monster, and I saw her expression change, flicker ever so slightly. If *this* legend was true...why *couldn't* there be a Blackbird King, a Blackbird Kingdom?

A blackbird girl?

"I don't know what could have happened to her," I said, when the darkness came, prowling along the roots of the trees, like the mist. Belinda struck a tinder stone, fed it to the tiny pile of sticks and needles she'd managed to gather together. "We have to wait for her."

"The first snowfall will be soon," she pointed out, gesturing overhead. "We have nothing with us. We're not prepared to withstand a winter out in these woods. We have to find shelter."

I sighed, leaned against the cold stones of the tower, crossing my arms and shivering. Oh, how I wished I'd tossed the stupid blanket from the stupid bed out the window. I was so piteously cold.

"Here," Belinda sighed, and she sat beside me, wrapped me in her cloak, too. We sat together, shaking, as the night opened up around us, black as hell.

"What if she's hurt somewhere?" I managed, teeth clacking. "What if...what if..." My stomach turned, and I rubbed at my eyes fiercely, willing myself not to cry.

Belinda cast me a sidelong glance, looked quickly back to the fire, but I had seen her expression. "What?" I asked. She shook her head.

"You truly love her," she said quietly. I breathed out, saw my breath come into the air, white and billowing, a cloud of heat.

"I do," I replied. I felt it, in that moment, felt it gathered and deep in my heart, the seed that was growing, changing into something else. It was the truth. I loved her.

And I needed to find her.

"We'll find her together," Belinda said, drawing out the words. "We'll find her."

"How can you be so sure?" I whispered, putting my terrible fear out into the world between us.

"I knew you were here," she said simply, looking down at her hands. "I knew I had to find you. I know she's out there."

I stilled at that, calmed. Belinda knew, had faith, trusted her instincts...hell, remembered how to *actually use them*.

I pillowed my head on her shoulder, shut my eyes, the fear laying down its own head, too, silenced.

"Thank you for coming for me," I told her then.

Belinda sighed. I could actually *feel* her rolling her eyes. "We stick together, yeah? Only next time--don't be so stupid, okay?"

"I'll try my best." I grinned.

"You'll do better than try, missy..."

I laughed, and she laughed, and the darkness was kept at bay with the world's tiniest, most pathetic fire.

*

I'm warmblooded, but after a night spent in half a threadbare cloak on almost-frozen ground, I was reaching the end of my ability to cope with the insipid, thrice-damned *cold*.

"Where should we go?" asked Belinda, when we'd more or less stomped out the fire, tossing a chunk of ice we'd found beside the tower wall on top of it. I rubbed my hands together, cast about, then looked up at the mounting sun.

"North," I decided. "That's where Merle said the Blackbird Kingdom is."

Belinda shook her head. "Don't you remember? In the legend, it says normal mortals will never be able to find it." She grimaced. "I don't know if that's true...but the other stuff has proved true so far. Can we risk it? If we miss the Blackbird Kingdom, it's just the mountains after that... We'll freeze to death."

I considered this, huffing white clouds out into the frozen morning. "Well..." I said, trying to think as quickly as I could.

Belinda pulled the needle out of her cloak, where she'd bent it to form a rusty clasp. It tugged now toward me, at the edge of its string. "I swear," she muttered, "I'm going to stick this in a tree. It's obnoxious when you're actually right here."

I stared at it. "You got that from that terrible magicmaker, right?"

Belinda nodded. "She scraped it against the hagstone, said your name three times... Really, I didn't feel like I was getting my money's worth, but..."

"Can you change what or who it's meant to find?"

Belinda shook her head. "It'll only work for you," she sighed. "That's what the spell was intended for."

I thought quickly. "But...she used a hagstone."

Belinda frowned. "That's what I said--"

"Can't we assume that the Haglin would have a hagstone? That's who they're named after! The Haglin could re-enchant it for us, and we could be off on our merry way to Merle, to the Blackbird Kingdom. It would *have* to direct us to the right place!"

Belinda was as white as newly driven snow. She shook her head furiously. "We can't find the Haglin! She's pure evil!"

"Evil!" I scoffed. "That's just a story."

"May I point out," Belinda hissed, "that-- thus far--all of these stories are proving *true*?"

"She's our only shot," I pointed out, to the woods. "They say she has her cottage here, in Bran Wood..."

"Bran Wood is a very big place," Belinda whispered, voice small. "We'll never find her, and we'll die, lost in the forest."

"When did you get so pessimistic?"

"When they came for you."

We both fell silent. I rubbed at my shoulders, stared at the ground.

"I'm sorry," I said then. "You don't...you don't know how sorry I am. I was stupid. It was all stupid. I never meant... I'm sorry." My voice cracked. "It's all shit now, isn't it? I've ruined everything."

Belinda breathed out, breath white, eyes wide. "No. It's not shit. We'll fix things."

"Thanks," I managed, turning my mouth up at the corners.

"So...which way do we go?"

I looked about us, picked a random direction and pointed at it, hoping my instincts were still intact.

We walked. When we thought we might be tired of walking, we walked some more. All morning, we trudged through the seemingly never-ending repetition of towering trees and random hillocks and valleys. I was so cold that I couldn't feel most of my face, my hands, my knees, my legs, my feet... I groaned when we stopped for what seemed like the twentieth time to jump up and down, flapping our arms and legs to stay warm.

That was Belinda's idea. Not mine.

"It's a cursed forest," said Belinda through chattering teeth. "That's what they say. Why do they say that?"

"And who's 'they'?" I muttered, shaking my head. "I don't know. I thought it was cursed because of Bran Tower, and the Haglin lives here... But, I mean, trappers live in the forest. Farmers..." I trailed off. People *lived* in the forest. It couldn't be so very cursed if they managed to survive here. There were people in the Angotha marketplace all the time who came from Bran Wood.

"Do you think..." Belinda licked her lips. "Do you think it's cursed to just make us wander in circles until we die?"

I snorted. "We're not going to *die*, Bels." It sounded flat, even to me.

We kept walking.

Twilight was falling, descending fast and hard like a stone, when Belinda touched my arm. I stopped, shaking so hard I wondered if I'd be able to keep standing. We had been walking the entire day, had seen nothing but repeating trees and unending bracken and moss. Maybe the wood really *was* cursed to make you wander forever. The thought gave me no comfort.

She pointed to the side. There, in the half light, something shone. A candle? Fire?

"Do you think it's a house?" I whispered around clacking teeth. Belinda shrugged, burrowed a little deeper in her cloak's hood.

"We have to go see," she said, inclining her head toward it. We crept through the twilit wood as the object of light drew closer. In the gloom, we could make out four walls made of logs, a pointed and steepled roof, smoke curling out of the chimney like fingers.

I stayed Belinda, grabbing hold of her cloak. "What if...what if..." A million possibilities of who and what could be inside that cabin in a cursed wood crawled through my mind. A thief is ever distrusting.

"What if what?" she asked, exasperated. "We're going to *die*, Envy. We have to get warm."

"You're obsessed with death," I muttered.

We crept up to the door.

"You knock," Belinda hissed, poking me in the ribs. I grimaced, shaking my head, but after another poke, I took a step closer to the door. I knocked, once, twice, thrice, biting my lip.

The door opened beneath my hand.

My first thought: she's *beautiful*.

My second thought: not as beautiful as Merle.

My third thought: she has a cat on her shoulder.

For the very pretty lady did, indeed, have a gray-striped tabby riding on her shoulder. The woman wore a simple cotton dress, like myself, with an apron over the skirt, perfectly spotless. She had long, wavy blonde hair that looked extraordinarily soft, and eyes so blue, they seemed to spark. Her perplexed expression warmed up to a smile when I grinned at her, exuding what I hoped to be charm and not frostbite.

"Hello, ma'am," I said humbly, spreading my hands. "We're just two weary travelers...um...traveling..." My tongue was so cold; I was stumbling over my words. Belinda coughed a little, stepped forward.

"We're lost, you see," she said, voice soft. "We were just wondering if we could sleep by your fire tonight."

"Of course!" said the woman, tone warm, husky, like she'd been singing all day. "Please come in, my dears. I am Maria."

We stepped inside, and she shut the door behind us. The cabin was small but so warm that I immediately began to feel my frozen appendages melting. Everything here was wooden, rustic, handhewn, from the table and chairs by the fire to the bed draped with a colorful quilt in the corner. There was a tall case of books, and a cauldron over the fire, and there were cats *everywhere*. The most smug cat sat on the woman's shoulder, blinking long and slow at us, but there were two more on the table, three curled up in little circles on the bed, and four in front of the fire.

"I can offer you supper," said the woman, crossing to the great cauldron. She stirred it briskly, tapping the spoon against the iron rim. "May I ask why you are wandering around in the woods in just a dress?" She raised an eyebrow in my direction. I blushed a little, but that could have just been myself melting some more.

"It's a long story," I said, and Belinda and I sat down on the floor before the great fire.

Gradually, my shaking eased to an occasional shiver. I let the fire warm my hands, my palms, my fingers. The heat was delicious. There were herbs burning in the blaze, and Maria threw on another bit of dried flowers, the scent strong but sweet...lavender? A cat crawled into my lap from the hearth, a great golden tabby. I pet her absentmindedly, feeling the purr to my bones and back.

"Now," said the woman, pulling her chair close to us. "Tell me your story."

Her gentle expression, her intense curiosity and the warmth of the fire *did* something to me. In some distant variation of horror, I realized that I was telling her the truth. All the while, as I spoke, the cat purred in my lap, and my hand stroked back and forth, petting down her golden fur.

"And I love her," I finished. "And I need to find her."

"Hm," was what the woman said, standing, stirring the pot. She rapped the wooden spoon against the metal rim again and went to her bookcase. It was piled with books, scrolls, bits of paper that fluttered down from the top shelf when she pulled out one of the fatter books, bringing it to the table.

"I remember Merle," said the woman, smiling. "She was a good girl. Not a rogue, like her father."

Belinda and I exchanged a glance, the color draining from both of our faces.

"Are you..." I tried, but she grinned down at both of us from her perch on the chair.

"You didn't guess?" she laughed a little, shaking her head, rueful. "I must be what you weren't expecting. But you, my dear Envy, should *always* expect the unexpected. Especially in Bran Wood." She turned open the gargantuan book, letting it settle in a cloud of great dust. "Now...let me see here..."

I blinked and opened and shut my mouth. "But you *cursed* them--"

She sighed, rolled her eyes heavenward. "That's just a story. I didn't curse them; what they stole did. They stole a cursed object. I mean, really, they might have expected it to have a bit of curse left in it. A great golden mirror," she smiled, holding up her hands to indicate how big it had been; her palms drifted three feet apart. "It had belonged to my stepmother, and she was such a wicked lady. But, yes, the Blackbird King stole it, and for his troubles, the curse descended upon him and his men...and his daughter. She was so nice, that Merle. No wonder you love her." She winked.

Well. I'd been taken to Bran Tower, had fallen in love with a blackbird girl... I could believe the Haglin was actually a charming woman in an apron and not an evil mastermind who ate little children. I yawned in spite of myself, already comfortable with the idea.

"Oh, you must be tired," she said, frowning. "We'll have supper, and then we'll discuss how you'll find her in the morning, if you'd like. Don't worry. I'll help you. I love a good love story."

She ladled out big spoonfuls of soup in roughly carved wooden bowls, and we ate so quickly our throats burned--not that it mattered. I was so hungry, I didn't even taste it.

"Now," she said, patting her knees, rubbing an affectionate knuckle on the purring cat who took up most of her lap. "You can take the bed if you like, my dears. It wouldn't be the first time I've slept in the rocker."

Belinda and I exchanged a glance. "Not that I want to...you know...ruin this entirely," I said, weariness making me drag out the words. "But if you're going to--oh, I don't know--turn evil in the middle of the night and start chopping us up for tomorrow's stew, can you kill us before we wake up?"

Maria laughed, the rich sound ringing like bells in the little cabin. "You folks from the city, you always expect the worse," she smiled, patting our shoulders. "Go to bed. I'm not going to kill or eat you. I doubt you'd taste very good."

I fell asleep before I hit the pillow.

I took her at her non-cannibalistic word.

*

After we devoured a spectacular breakfast of bits-of-apple in porridge, Maria stretched overhead and shooed the two cats who had taken up residence on her lap down to the floor.

"I consulted my great book," she said companionably, steepling her fingers. "And I know just what to do to help you find your way to the Blackbird Kingdom. Sadly, a simple needle charm like yours, Belinda, will not work when the place is hidden by a curse. So! We have our work cut out for us!" Her smile was huge, and only slightly scary.

"What sort of work?" I asked, brow furrowed. The Haglin rose, took her heavily embroidered cloak from the peg by the door. It was covered in small strawberries and moons. She handed it to me.

"We have to dig up a body," she said, smile never wavering.

I dropped the cloak.

Maria, of course, had three shovels. And an extra cloak for herself. We followed her down an almost imperceptible path through Bran Wood, her shovel held easily on her shoulder.

"You see, if you wish to find an enchanted place, you must arrive in an enchanted way. The rules of magic are actually quite logical. Something earned must have something taken, something found must have something lost, and something created must have something destroyed. Nature balances herself out so well!" she veritably sang. Belinda and I exchanged a glance.

"So, what we must do," said Maria pausing for a minute, turning this way and that, nose upturned to the sky, "is create an enchanted transportation for you. And, believe it or not, this is the easiest way I can think of. I consulted the soup cauldron last night after you went to bed," she said, throwing a glance over her shoulder. "I saw your Merle."

"In...in the soup cauldron?" I was so completely confused at the same time as my heart thundered.

"Sort of," she answered without hesitation. "Not *in* the soup cauldron, but *through* the soup cauldron. I use it as an augury, much more useful than a crystal ball or scrying mirror, just cluttering the place up. Anyway," she continued, licking her finger and holding it up to the wind, "it seems that she's been kidnapped."

"*What*?" I hissed, reeling as the Haglin set off in a new direction, replacing her glove. I dropped the shovel, raced ahead, touched her arm. "Please..." I murmured, heart pounding against my bones. "What...what do you mean, *kidnapped*?"

Maria's face softened. "It seems that a band of brigands set their sights on the tower, and they saw her coming and going, saw her shapechange...put two and two together. Though how those thugs managed to figure anything out is quite beyond me. They seem vastly stupid." She rolled her eyes. "But they kidnapped her when she changed that night, in the woods. They're holding her for ransom to the Blackbird King. They want his treasure, or they will kill her."

I didn't know what to do. I couldn't breathe, couldn't think, couldn't stand. I knelt, suddenly, head in hands, feeling my heart pound, feeling my breath come in slight gusts, trembling, every inch of me trembling.

"You cannot help her this way," said the Haglin gently, crouching down beside me. "And I believe that you *can* help her, Envy. You are very brave of heart. Women who are brave of heart have heaven and earth move for them, it seems. Be brave."

I looked up at her brows furrowed, her eyes bright and clear, blue as morning. "Be brave," she repeated, nodding. I nodded, too, standing, swallowing. I felt sick.

Be brave.

When the first shovel hit the dirt, it made a sound like metal against metal, a sharp note that rang against the trees, crouched and waiting around us.

We three dug. My palms, bloodied from the previous day, began to leak through the fabric wound about them. They stained the rough wooden handle of the shovel a dirty red. I bit my lip, the pain grafting itself along my arms to my shoulders to my heart, splintering there.

The earth and my hands smelled like metal. When my shovel hit something softer than the frozen earth, I almost didn't notice--in fact, lowered the shovel again.

It stuck. I pulled, and pulled, and the shovel came up, along with something viciously red against the dark earth.

Blood welled out of the tiny break in the ground. I stared, panting.

"Out of the hole," said Maria crisply, helping both Belinda and me up and out. I scrambled, for the red welled up faster than I would have thought possible, kissing the bottom of my slippers before I sat on the edge of the hole we'd dug, heart pounding, watching blood fill the cavity.

"Good," the Haglin whispered. "This is good. He wants life again. This will be easier than I thought. Now, Envy," she said, crouching beside me. "Envy, will you be brave still, dear girl?"

"I don't understand," I muttered, but she pressed her dirty finger to my lips. I tasted iron.

"I would give you what you need to find the Blackbird Kingdom, but it is not mine to give. There must be a take in magic that gives--do you understand?"

"No," I said. The blood was beginning to pool up and over the edge of the hole, flowing for us.

"He won't live without a heart," said Maria. "In order for the spell to be sealed, you must give your heart in exchange."

I stared at her, uncomprehending. "That's not possible--"

"The spell will last for thirteen days. If you can get him back in thirteen days, your heart will be returned to you, good as new. You won't even miss it. If you don't return in time...you will die."

I breathed out, closed my eyes. I heard the blood welling, bubbling. I was going to be sick.

"Nothing comes without price," Maria whispered. "Do you agree to give your heart, Envy?"

I opened my eyes.

I had to find Merle.

"Yes."

It was painless. Maria withdrew an apple from her satchel, held it out to me. Tentatively, I took it, and it disappeared the moment it touched my skin. And in Maria's flattened palm lay something quivering, beating, red.

I supposed that was my heart. I pressed my hand against my breast. I felt no different.

"The apple keeps the spot in your chest from decaying," she muttered, turning to look at the pool of blood at our feet. "All right. Let's see now..." And the heart slipped from her fingers into the hole.

It splashed, the blood sputtering up and around us. At first, nothing happened. The hush and rush of the blood kept on; everything tasted like metal, the bright red a dizzying color in the dulled gray of an almost-winter forest.

And then a roar leaped up from the hole, surrounded us like air, a heavy bellow that made us cover our ears with our hands, cry out. I thought the earth was quaking, thought it would swallow us whole, and it was true--the earth was *shaking*. I cried out just as silence descended.

It stood on the edge of the hole, sides heaving. It was horse-shaped but mostly bones and sinew and muscle, and it looked like something you'd see hanging outside of the tannery, not at all like a living thing, standing before us on three-and-a-half feet. It swiveled a great, decaying head toward us, fixed a milky blue eye on Maria.

"Hello, Satin," she whispered.

The thing shook its head, pawed the earth with a hoof, skin dripping down its leg. "Why have you brought me back?" it asked, lifting up its head, clacking its teeth like a shiver. "Why?"

"You're needed, my beautiful boy," said Maria, rising. She held out her hand to him, and he stepped forward once, twice, pushed his nose against her palm.

"I was so tired," he said, shaking his head, then. "I wanted to sleep forever."

"I hope you will forgive me," she said, and I noticed her sorrowful face, heard the pain in her tone. She gazed at the gaping holes along his flanks, the way the bone and muscle worked in concert. She looked away.

"This is Satin. He was my horse once. He was the most faithful friend I've ever had," she said, and she carefully laid a hand on his flank. He shuddered beneath her touch, and where her fingers rested, skin began to unfurl like ribbons. As we watched, skin and a bright, burnished fur the color of a tongue began to cover him, spiraling out from her hand.

He raised his head to bellow to the heavens. For a moment, we saw the magnificent beast that had once been, a stallion, and then Maria removed her hand, and he was reduced again to bones and sinew and only one great, unseeing eye.

"You must carry these young ladies to the Blackbird Kingdom, my beauty," she whispered to Satin, placing her arms about his neck. He lowered his head, flaps of skin shifting in the wind that had begun moving across the puddle of blood left in the hole.

"Thirteen days," she managed, not able to look at either of us. There were tears in her eyes, on her cheeks. "He must be back in thirteen days, or the heart will fail, and he will die again, and you will, too, Envy."

"Thank you," I whispered, holding out my arms to her, and we embraced as the first snowflake danced down from the heavens, and it began: winter.

Maria handed us a satchel filled with food, and then she knelt down beside Satin on one knee, holding out her hand to us. "I'll help you up."

I grimaced, stepping on her knee as quickly as I could, throwing myself up and onto the back of the dead animal, purely graceless. Belinda followed behind me, gripping my waist. There was nothing for me to hold, save for his shoulder bone, which I did, trying not to think about what I was doing.

"Take care of them," she told the great beast, and he nodded, raising his head to the sky.

"Be brave!" Maria called after us, and then Satin shuddered and moved through the woods as fast as any beast of hell.

*

Having ridden on a rotten horse, I can say, in all honestly, it's not too terrible.

We kept sliding off to the right, which was a bit awkward, but we'd rarely ridden horses in our day-to-day lives as very poor thieves and then very poor maids. It really had nothing to do with the fact that Satin had no mane to grip onto.

He ran smoothly between the trees, the methodic *ba-da-dum, ba-da-dum* of his feet almost soothing. We rode this way until sundown.

We were drifting nearer to the northern mountain range of Sapphira. Glimmer Mountain was the closest mountain to us, rising out of the darkness, towering over the forest pines. You could tell it was Glimmer Mountain because of the gentle-sloped peak--the only one not steepled at the top. I peered up and back, amazed by its snowy head up close...or closer. It was so magical, so beautiful, the way it looked like a gently spread blanket, soft and inviting.

If the stories were right, being so close to the mountains meant that we were close to the Blackbird Kingdom, too. But *were* the stories right? The Haglin was hardly the sadistic old woman of legend, just a really nice lady who liked cats and helping people. And there hadn't been someone cursing someone else, only a set of circumstances that might be chalked up to bad luck. I knew a thing or two about bad luck.

Satin paused, lifting up his nose to the heavens. The first stars of evening were blossoming in the sky; the sun had set. It was so abysmally cold, not even Maria's lovely cloak could keep my teeth from chattering. Satin's bones were cold, too, which wasn't helping.

"We're close to Night Village," he said then.

"What's that?" I asked. Actually, it came out more like this: "Wha-at's...tha-at...?" I couldn't speak around my frozen tongue, but Satin got the gist of it. He snorted.

"Night Village is on the border of the Blackbird Kingdom. It guards the Nightmare Gate, which is how you enter the kingdom," he said, turning back and regarding us with one baleful blue eye. "I'll help you find it, and then I'll get through the gate. Which, as you might guess, is quite a nightmare."

I snorted. The magical, talking dead horse had a dry sense of humor.

Belinda poked me in the ribs. "What?" I managed, over my shoulder, as Satin began to walk down a hillock at a sedate pace in the darkening woods.

"That doesn't sound very safe," she managed. Her teeth were chattering, too. "Nightmare Gate?"

I shook my head. None of this added up to my favorite way to spend a night--but I had to find Merle.

I had no idea where the brigands who had kidnapped Merle could be. If I found the Blackbird King, though, he would know. It was a terrible plan, but it was something, and I needed to do *something*.

I had to find her.

The dark crawled along the roots of trees, dragging itself across the forest floor until night had fallen. It was so gradual that I was surprised when the velvet blackness became absolute. The clouds had built up steadily all afternoon, and toward evening, the sky had been threatening snow. Now, in the hush of the woods, snow began to fall, the cold insipid and sharp. Wolflike.

"Are you very cold?" asked Satin after a long while. I couldn't feel any part of my body. That was a resounding *yes*. I tried to tell him so but couldn't force out the word.

"Get down," he said gently, and we did, falling in a heap into the forgiving snow. It was now coming down fast, the flakes so thick, I could hardly see Belinda, as close as she was, huddled near me for warmth.

Satin lay down, letting out a great *whoosh* of breath. "Come closer. I'll see what I can do," he told us. We did as we were asked, curling up in the spiral of his hooves.

He curved his great head toward us and breathed out. I had been struggling against sleep for most of the evening, but now I succumbed, going under as easily as when Merle had said, "Sleep."

She was my last thought before I drifted away.

*

Everything was silent when I opened my eyes. Silent and white. I blinked, worked my jaw up and down, sitting up. The snow slid off of me in a great pile, and the light of morning pervaded everything. The sun was nowhere to be seen; the clouds still banked up on the horizon, over us like a dome. But we had survived a winter's night.

"It was magic?" I asked the horse as I stood, as I helped Belinda stand. I felt perfectly all right-- warm, even. Belinda shook out her cloak, looked about her in wonder. Satin stood, too, shaking like a newborn colt.

"Yes, magic," he acquiesced, turning up his nose again. "We must ride now. You must get to Night Village by afternoon if we are to make it to the Nightmare Gate by twilight. That's the only time it opens." He knelt down carefully, and I managed to crawl onto his back with only a minor loss of dignity. I helped Belinda up behind me, and we rode on.

Perhaps there was more magic, for the day passed much warmer than the previous one. Perhaps it was simply hope. Satin slowed in his headlong gallop in the late afternoon. The sun already descending rapidly toward the horizon. He raised his head to sniff the air.

"Just over the ridge," he said, nodding toward the north.

And there it was.

Night Village was a tiny grouping of homes, all snow-covered, like a charming painting, forming one road with a crossroad for the village. We crested the hillock and stared down at the smoke curling from the chimneys, at the people moving through the two streets like dolls. Near the far end of the village, where the larger road led, stood a great crowd of pine trees, trees taller than Bran Tower itself, it seemed. I had never seen anything so tall, tall enough to gather the stars. They almost formed a gateway, with a natural opening amidst the tree trunks.

"Night Village," said Satin, nodding. "And Nightmare Gate."

We descended the hill slowly. It was more like a tiny mountain than a hill, anyway, so close to the mountain range; the going was a bit hard on Satin. He braced his haunches and skidded down some inclines, Belinda and I leaning back so far that we might have toppled off backwards if I hadn't been clutching onto his shoulder bones. Finally, the ground leveled out, and we were on the straightaway to the village.

People spotted us; there was arm waving aplenty, and a small crowd gathered by the time we reached the street's mouth.

"Satin," said a man, looking up at the horse with a smile. He had thin lips and an orange cloak wrapped about him. When he shifted, I stared terribly, mouth open. One arm wasn't an arm...but a wing.

"I am flattered that you still know me, John," said the horse, bowing his head. "John, this is Envy and Belinda. They have business with the Blackbird King."

"Welcome to Night Village," said John, and when he looked up and smiled at us, I knew he meant it. "We aren't exactly part of the Blackbird Kingdom...but we almost are. We're the beginning." And he nodded up at us, at Satin. "If you like, you can wait inside until nightfall. We don't have much, but you're welcome to come to the village meetinghouse." He turned, and Satin followed him into town.

I tried my best not to stare at the other residents, but I couldn't help it. There was a woman with a cat nose and whispers and ears; there was a man with the head of a stork. There was a woman with a flicking tongue. All of these people had aspects that were distinctly animal-like.

"You are curious," said John, when we reached the only square in the village, when we dismounted Satin. I blushed, but Belinda smiled.

"We come from Angotha," she said, as if that was explanation enough.

"We are all cursed," said John with a grin. I blanched, but he laughed a little. "It's not nearly so terrible as all that, Miss Envy. We have various aspects of the Major Curse that created the Blackbird King. So, somehow, all of us misfits were drawn together, sought him out... Night Village is the border of the Blackbird Kingdom, and the Blackbird King is very kind. He takes care of us here. And we, in turn, protect the gateway." He pointed up the road, at the towering pine trees. "But come inside! Warm yourselves!" He held the door open for us, and even Satin, who clopped up the two short steps with considerable dexterity.

Once inside, I sat by the fire, holding out my hands to it. I sat back in alarm when I realized there was a small woman dancing in the blaze.

"A flame siren," said John, squatting next to me. "She won't hurt you. She's just interested in you."

She stood about two feet tall, a perfect miniature. She smiled up at me, lips flickering. Her entire body was made of flame.

"We are the magical misfits of the world, you see," said John. "There's a place for everyone here, thanks to the Blackbird King. You'll see him soon enough," he added. "You can get into his kingdom only at twilight. It's how the curse works."

"Have you...have you seen Merle?" I asked him, my voice breaking on the word. I cursed myself. I couldn't cry. He looked at me strangely, brow furrowed.

"She was kidnapped by a band of ragtag thieves, I hear. Terrible ones, I might add. They caught her when she was just changed, and she couldn't defend herself." His one hand curled into a tight fist. "They are holding her for ransom. They wish to exchange all of the Blackbird King's treasures for her life. But it is not so easy as that. Ragla fears that if he hands over his treasures, they will still kill her. They are witless, but they are cruel." John's kind face was lined with grief. "How do you know about her, our Merle?" he asked then.

So I told him.

His face shone, and he had to rise toward the end of my tale, drawing other people in from the village, as I recounted bits and pieces of it all over again. Their happiness was infectious. They were overjoyed at our love, overjoyed that their blackbird princess had found a bride.

It had come to that, hadn't it? No matter what happened, that's who I was now.

The blackbird girl's bride.

I had to find her. I had to help her. I had to save her. It ate at me, that pervasive worry, eating up my hopes, my joy, my happiness at their happiness. As twilight approached, John sobered, too, and we left the great, warm meetinghouse, all of us, moved out into the darkening streets.

"Nightmare Gate isn't so bad," said John, as we walked toward the pine trees. The people of Night Village walked with us.

The man with a stork's head--George--nodded. "Night Village is impossible for normal mortals to find. As you can see, we are not normal mortals," he grinned, his beak rounding at the corners. "Satin helped you find this place. Without him, without his magic, you wouldn't be here. But since we are at risk for invasion by various magicmakers, Nightmare Gate was put in place as the final threshold before the Blackbird Kingdom."

"It is a gate of pure darkness. A darkness so absolute that it terrifies those who don't know its secret, and they cannot cross it," said John. "But you will know its secret, and you will be just fine. The secret is that, five steps forward, you will find light. The darkness is not forever. Five steps. Five steps, and you will be in the Blackbird Kingdom."

Belinda gripped my hand so tightly, I couldn't feel my fingers. "It's all right, Bels," I told her quietly. We'd gotten close to the trees now. The villagers stood on the edge of pine needles, smiling their encouragement to us.

"Whatever is decided--if you need our help..." John trailed off. "Please know we would do anything for our Merle."

I believed him. I smiled, bowed my head to them.

"We'll...see you soon," I said, and--one hand on Satin's bone shoulder, the other gripped tightly by Belinda--I stepped into the ring of pine trees.

It was instant, the black that descended, such an utter, complete black that I believed I had never known darkness, true darkness, in all my days. Belinda's nails dug into my palm, but I squeezed tighter, took another step. I couldn't breathe, couldn't see, couldn't imagine venturing another step, but there was one more step, and one more step after that, and we stumbled from perfect, pure black to a blaze and riot of color. I breathed.

We were in a cobblestone hallway that stretched on into the distance, guttering torches highlighting the tapestries that covered the walls. Tapestries of people dancing around trees with ribbons, and unicorns and apples and maidens, and they were never-ending in their depictions of joy and happiness. A plush rug of crimson rolled away on the floor, and Satin looked very out of place, and shabby--a fact that made me want to hug him about the neck. Which I might have done at that moment. But he lowered his big head against my shoulder and sighed.

"We must find the Blackbird King," he said. "This corridor leads to his throne room. Let us follow it."

We walked the rug forever (or so it seemed), until the hallway opened up all of the sudden after we rounded a bend. A throne room spread before us now, but it so different from King Allefred's. His throne room was austere, cold, built of carved marble. This space had warm wooden walls, more tapestries, a big, overstuffed chair that stood at one end of the room on a dais-- presumably the throne, though it was the most non-royal throne I had ever seen.

And on the throne sat a man. He stood when we entered the room, as if two strange woman and a rotting horse stumbled into his throne room at all sorts of odd hours. His hair was black and sharp, his eyes flashing, and his smile wide. He reminded me of Merle.

He was the Blackbird King. He spread his arms, and then he was embracing me.

He knew me.

He held me out at arm's length, still silent, and it was then that I noticed the tears in his eyes. "You made her so happy," he said, his eyes so like hers that I was weeping, and we held each other for a long moment, connected.

"I am Ragla," he said, eventually, drying his tears on the corner of his cloak. "I am the Blackbird King, and--I assure you--I am not usually so at wit's end. Have you any news of my daughter, Envy? Do you know any more?" He searched my face, and I had to shake my head. His disappointment was palpable.

"These are my friends," I said, clearing my throat. "This is Belinda, and this is Satin."

"Hello, Belinda," said the king tiredly, though his smile was genuine. "And hello again, Satin. Good to see you, old friend."

I sat down on the edge of the raised platform of his throne, rubbing at my eyes.

"What can you tell me about the brigands?" I asked him. He shrugged, climbed up the platform, too, to sit on his throne.

"They sent me a letter of ransom," he said, words breaking. "They are somewhere in Bran Wood, and they have my daughter. But the terrible thing...the worst *possible* thing is that they have no mercy. I know this--I know them. I believe that if I do give them my entire treasure-- what does it matter to me, giving them my treasure? I would do it in a heartbeat--that they will still kill my daughter."

"But aren't you immortal?" I asked, desperate. He shook his head.

"We are immortal here, within the confines of my kingdom," he said, his voice small. "Outside, we can be killed."

Perhaps that had been my last hope. It felt like it. I wanted to curl up, to weep until there were no longer tears in me, and sleep until I felt nothing. I put my head in my hands, pressed my fingers to my eyes, a riot of violet blossoming in the darkness.

Merle could be killed.
She could die.

"Be brave, Envy," said Satin gently. "Maria would not have sent me if she thought it an impossible task."

That was something. I sighed, straightened, hands at the small of my back. "Do you know where they are now...with Merle?"

The king frowned. "Though I have much magic at my disposal, they're using cloaking spells. Terrible ones," he twisted his mouth wryly, "but they're working well enough to evade me, so I suppose they're not without merit. I do know that the northwestern edge of Bran Wood is impossible for me to read currently--so they are somewhere there."

I kneaded my forehead, tried to think. "Do you have...oh, I don't know, men? Do you have guards? Soldiers?"

He nodded, then sighed. "I do, but if the brigands see them approach, they'll kill her instantly. It's too great a risk."

In the far-off reaches of my mind, I realized that--like Merle--the king was easy to talk to, kind. I wondered what he would be like, under other circumstances, realized that I liked him very much. I hoped I would get a chance to know him better, by Merle's side.

Oh, Merle... I felt the tears come again and stomped them down. No. Not now. I had to *think*. I was clever; I could be even more clever. I could think of a solution.

The king roused himself, face apologetic. "Are you hungry? I can fix you supper... Are you

cold? Ah, me, I'm a terrible host. Forgive me..."
 And then he whistled a tune, and three guards
stepped into the room, bowed. I assumed they
were guards, though they weren't wearing any
sort of armor, were simply dressed in black pants
and tunics. Their brows were furrowed, their faces
expectant. With a single glance, I knew they
adored their king.

I began to see that the stories of the good
Blackbird King could be true.

"Please bring something warm and tasty for
our new guests? I'm so sorry to ask, but they just
arrived," said Ragla, holding out his hands to us.
 The men nodded quickly, offering us fast grins
before departing.

"Please, dear ladies," said Ragla then,
"come with me to the dining hall. We will all
think better on full stomachs." Satin followed
behind us, hooves ringing out eerily when we
crossed from the carpeted floors to wooden ones,
polished to a mirror-like gleam. They shone in the
dim torchlight.

Is this where Merle had spent her days,
walking through these corridors, hand along these
walls? If I closed my eyes, it was very easy to
imagine her here, her steps ringing over the
floorboards, smiling and ready and waiting to
greet me with a kiss.

Ragla laid a hand on my shoulder, the
weight comforting. "Now that you're here, I think
things will go better," he said, words quiet. "I
prayed to Goddess Luck, you know. I prayed that

an answer would come. I think you can help my daughter, Envy. You already have, so much. She loves you..." His voice cracked. "I've never seen her this happy," he finished. "Thank you."

I didn't know what to say, cleared my throat. "She makes me very happy, too," I said. "I've never...I've never been happier."

"That's how you know," he said simply.

He was right.

The dining hall was much smaller than King Allefred's but cozy, warm, with golden tapestries draped over the walls stitched with blackbirds. There were several people seated at the tables, and they brought their dishes in and out of the door that I assumed must lead to the kitchen. I watched in fascination. It took me a long moment to realize...no servants? This was a very different kingdom, indeed.

Two guards brought us bowls of soup, and after I slurped down the hot broth, my thief fingers had to resist the urge to stuff the bowl down my shirt. It was made of a faceted type of glass I'd never seen before. It sparkled. Belinda and I stared at our bowls in wonder, and Ragla noticed, laughing.

"We are blackbirds, essentially," he winked. "We enjoy shiny things."

Of course.

We devoured the soup quickly, and with Satin curled up in a corner of the room, Ragla brought out a great map, spreading it on the table before us. The parchment was expertly marked with dotted lines, tiny trees and mountain ranges. I stared, transfixed. Here was Sapphira, in miniature.

"I'm William," said one of the men who had brought us the soup. His eyes were wide-set and brown and mischievous, though their flash subdued as he pointed to the northwestern edge of the map. "I've flown over this area. I went there again today. I have reason to believe that the brigands are there, using camouflage to prevent me from spotting them. There was a particularly magical scent to the air. I do believe they're there," William said, glancing up at Ragla, who nodded.

"That's what my scrying tells me, too," he said, chin in hands, gazing at the map. "I have, literally, thought of every other possibility to save her and discarded it," he told us. "I was going to send one of the Changers, the shapeshifters, there. I was going to send John, from the village. I thought the element of surprise might help us bring Merle back, and then I thought to just give them part of the treasure, get her back, and then give them all of the treasure... But the demands of the note are very precise. They must have all of the treasure by tomorrow evening, or they will slit her throat until dead." His voice wavered on the last part, and I glanced up, horrified.

"Tomorrow night? That's...that's less than twenty-four hours!" I groaned. "That's not enough time."

"I know," he muttered, turning the map this way and that. "We no longer have any choice.

Now we must go to the site specified in the ransom note--Bran Tower."

I held my head in my hands, pulled at my hair, did my absolute best to *think*. Mercenary brigands had Merle. Those sorts of people could not be moved by pleadings for compassion; they could not be moved by promises, for they never held to their word. They could be moved by money and power and treasure and...

I breathed out. And treasure.

The mirror.

I gasped, banging on the table so loudly that everyone jumped. "I'm sorry," I muttered. "The magic mirror that you stole from Maria-- where is it?"

Ragla frowned. "In one of the treasure rooms, surely. I'm...not certain. Why?"

"It's cursed, isn't it?"

William and Ragla exchanged a glance. "Yes..." said the Blackbird King, drawing out the word.

"I mean..." I spread my hands along the tabletop, desperate. "Couldn't it be used to curse *them*? The brigands?"

Ragla remained silent for a very long moment. "Curses are quite dangerous things," he said then, slowly. "If something went wrong...if any aspect of it went wrong, Merle could be doubly cursed. I'm not certain what would happen--"

"What is the curse, exactly?"

Ragla shook his head. "No one knows. It appears that this mirror used to change people into hedgehogs, of all things. There are so many stories about it that no one knows the truth. What I believe is that there are several curses set within the mirror, and they just come out...*randomly.*" He spread his hands. "Maria's told me what a sadistic person her stepmother was. I wouldn't doubt that she intended the mirror to behave in this erratic manner."

I bit my lip. The curses were volatile...unpredictable. This put quite a damper on the very fast, very ludicrous plan I was trying to cobble together. I opened and shut my mouth, cleared my throat.

"But...but what if it *did* work?"

"What are you getting it?" asked Ragla, eyebrow raised.

"What if I took the mirror with me--"

He shook his head. "You can't touch it. You'll be cursed."

"Well, then...on a horse cart. Satin could pull it!"

From the corner, my undead steed snorted but made no objection.

"And then...if the leader of the brigands--or, really, *any* of the brigands--touched it, they would all be cursed. I'd take Merle away, bring her back safe and sound, triumphant entrance, the end," I said, joy making my words slur together.

The others at the table considered my suggestion.

"So much might go wrong," said Ragla slowly. "They could be cursed with the *oddest* curse. It might not make them immobile, just angry. You would die, then."

"In the confusion, no matter what sort of curse comes out, I could grab Merle. I'm a thief," I told Ragla shyly. "I can pick locks. I'm not a very *good* thief, but I would find a way to get to Merle, to save her."

"I don't think it should be you who goes," said Ragla. "*I* should go..."

"We cannot lose you, sire," said William, shaking his head.

"I'm the obvious choice. They won't notice me. I'm no one of consequence. I blend in," I told him, pleading. "I can do this. I will save her. I *must* save her. Let me try."

Ragla sighed, gazed deeply into my eyes, searching. "These are very unkind men, Envy," he said. "They will not hesitate to slaughter you if they think you have tricked them."

"I have been told," I said, smile turning the corners of my mouth, "that they are also very stupid. And I am charming, and I am clever. These are my gifts. Let me use them. If they find out that I have double-crossed them, they will kill *me*, not her... They may still wait for the ransom. You might have another chance."

"We don't have much time, Ragla," said William, then, his voice strained. The king buried his face in his hands, tugged at his hair.

"If the roles were reversed," said the king after a very long time, "Merle would be doing exactly what you are doing, Envy. If you must venture forth...you are welcome to. Though I don't like it," he added, when I grinned from ear to ear, nodding so fast my head might have fallen off.

"Now we have only to find the mirror," he said, standing. "The brigands are bringing Merle with them to Bran Tower, because," his mouth twisted, "that's the only place they can find easily in all of Bran Wood. Not surprising."

I thought of the tower, cold and sad and lonely now that I'd gone. How, within those stone walls, so much had happened. So much had begun. I tapped my fingers against my lips, thinking quickly. "Will we be able to get there in time, do you think?"

"If you leave by tomorrow morning, yes," said the king. "We have the evening to find the mirror. Don't worry," he smiled, patting my arm. "You'll get there in time." A shadow was over his face. It was disconcerting, having someone concerned about me.

"I'll go with you," said Belinda, then. She'd been quiet during the conversation, hands on the table, fingers spread. Her eyes were flashing, and her mouth was in that particularly stubborn set that meant she was immovable on something.

"You *can't*," I spluttered. "Bels, you could die--"

"So could you," she said, tone defiant. "I lost you once, and I will be absolutely thrice damned if I let you trot off to rescue your girl without so much as a friend by your side. Don't be ridiculous," she said, words as firm as stone. "I am coming with you."

"The pack animal doesn't get much say," muttered Satin, rising to his feet, but his one good eye gave me a long, slow wink. "It's been quite awhile since I pulled a cart. I might have forgotten how to be mannerly."

I patted his shoulder bone, laughing. "I might have forgotten that as well. We'll make a fine team of rescuers." There was a lump in the back of my throat as I said it, fear circling my stomach like wolves. But I couldn't think that we'd fail. I had to believe that all of this had happened for some spectacular reason, that things would be okay...that, for once in my life, a happily ever after was within my reach, and it would *not* be snatched away by a flippant fate.

I had to believe that. And, as I did my absolute best to believe it, I realized that I had finally begun to believe in *something*.

The seed of love had grown, tall and wild in my heart, and now other things were growing. *Nice* things.

I followed Ragla down the corridors, leading deeper and deeper into his palace, and I sank just as deep in thought. When we reached the first storeroom and he opened the unlocked door, I was jolted out of my reverie by the base *shininess* of the room. I had never seen so much sparkle in my life.

"This is a hundred years of thievery, these storerooms. I have very bad collector tendencies," he laughed, "but I do seem to recall that the very thing that led to all of this Blackbird King and Kingdom nonsense was kept here, in this first room."

Which wouldn't exactly have been a problem if the storeroom was of a normal size. But it wasn't.

It seemed to stretch on forever.

The flash of gold and silver and gem and jewel almost blinded me as the torches lit within the room. Ragla strode in and down the very slim corridor between the aisles. Belinda and I followed. We seemed to have lost Satin, but he wouldn't have fit in here, anyway. We barely fit, and only sideways, holding in our stomachs. I could scarcely draw in a breath.

The king began to climb a pile of gold coins. They slid beneath him, and he slid down, too, but he doggedly continued until he got to the top. He reached into the pile, digging around this way and that, moving aside coins like one would small pebbles. My legs were buried almost up to my knees by the time he shouted "aha!" and tugged at something in the pile. It gave way, but so did the coins, and he skidded down on his backside, almost toppling us.

He held a mirror. It was large, almost as wide as a doorway, with gilt paint and an elaborate frame circling its silver center. I stared at it, transfixed. The mirrored part wasn't glass so much as...well, it seemed to be liquid silver. I reached forward--

"Mustn't," muttered the king, holding it out of my reach as we all struggled to stand. "Sadly, it's bewitched to draw you in." He took off his cloak and covered it, and suddenly I could breathe again. I sighed, long and low. Belinda rubbed at her eyes.

"Do not look at its surface directly," said the king, tucking the cloak-wrapped mirror under his arm. "Promise me?"

We promised. I, for once, did not cross my fingers.

There was a small horse cart, hardly big enough for the seat in the front that would hold Belinda and me, in the courtyard. The Blackbird Kingdom, Ragla told us, was a pocket of Sapphira that was simply hidden away--like a wrinkle in the land. There were stars overhead, and the moon. I didn't feel that we were in any sort of strange, otherworldly place, and the king agreed that we were not. That was comforting and also...exhilarating. Did this mean that there were other wrinkles across the world, just waiting to be discovered? I'd never thought on such things before.

My daydreams involving hidden lands and discovering them with Merle evaporated as we began to load up the cart--first with gold coins, then larger treasures like gold cups (oh, it was difficult to actually set them down, let them go) and plates and crowns. Apparently, Ragla liked

crowns a lot. The mirror had to be positioned at
the edge of the cart, not so close to the edge that it
might fall out and shatter, just close enough that,
when the brigands came to examine the treasure, it
would be the first thing they'd touch. As the sky
began to lighten, the sun pondering rising again
for another day, I sat on the edge of the cart, tried
to keep my eyes open. I was so very tired, but fear
was whispering in my heart... So much depended
upon this one, single day.

I had to stop thinking about it. I rubbed at
my eyes, hunkered down deeper into my cloak.
Merle. Tonight, I would see Merle. And I would
save her. I had to save her. There was no choice.
There would be no other chance.

This was...*it*. Oh, gods, I was going to be
sick.

"Ready?" asked Ragla, when the cart was
ready, when Satin had been hitched up in the
ridiculously embroidered and far-too-fancy
harness. There was actually a drooping feathered
plume at the top of the harness's bridle. On the
rotting horse, it...well, it would certainly surprise
the brigands, I supposed.

I gave Ragla a quick hug, could not look
him in the eyes. I knew I would cry, and, really, I
could not afford to do so again. I climbed up on
the cart seat, next to Belinda.

Ragla cleared his throat, looked up at the
both of us, clasped my hand. "There's nothing I
can say..." he murmured, but he nodded,

swallowed. "Thank you for trying. Goddess Luck smile on you."

I felt the warmth of the clay sun over my heart. I pressed my own hand there, nodded.

So we began, cart trundling through the palace gate, into pure blackness, and then beyond.

*

Satin moved as swiftly as he could, but the forest floor was knotty and strewn with roots, and the cart rumbled, dangerously close to tipping over at times. It was a very slow, very agonizing journey that we made through Bran Wood on our way back to the tower.

As the day went on, I occasionally got glimpses of the tower, when we crested hills and the trees thinned--there, in the distance, windows shining. Perversely, the sun was out and merry, and it was a warm day, or as warm as winter could offer. The snow that had fallen dazzled, and I pushed back my cloak's hood, too warm.

There was little conversation as we rode along, and I almost wished we had something light to talk about. If we failed...we would die. I bit my lip, gripped the cart's seat a bit harder over bumps--knuckles white--and tried to think about absolutely, positively nothing.

And absolutely failed.

The sun began to fall. The tower loomed closer. The afternoon slipped away.

And I prayed, over and over and over again: "Let me be brave, let me be clever. Let me be brave, let me be clever. If there was *ever* a time that I was brave and clever, let it be now."

The sun died.

And we arrived.

The tower's clearing was just as I half-remembered it. But there was a large fire now, flickering and crackling, and around it sat five men in tattered garments. Beside them was a large cage, and within the cage, there was a blackbird that changed from bird to girl even as we watched, as the sun slipped away. We had reached the brigand's camp.

And there was Merle. Merle, who sat on the bottom of the cage, eyes wide, fingers gripping the bars, mouth moving, speaking, too quiet for me to hear.

The largest man, who I supposed to be the leader, rose, nose to the air, eyes wide, too. I hopped down from the cart, came up beside Satin and put a hand on his shoulder. He was imposing, surprising. I hoped the sight of him would be enough to take these brigands off their guard.

"We have come from the Blackbird King with the ransom for Mer...the Blackbird Princess," I said, cursing myself at the correction. "Please come and examine the ransom so that we can take her and be done with all this foolishness."

The big man--why did it have to be the *big* man?--snorted.

"The Blackbird King is a thief. He's tricksy," he said, his accent that of a northlander. "Bring the cart closer."

I bit my lip. "Certainly," I said, and Satin and I moved toward them. The men stood hastily, moved away from the fire as Satin came to loom in their midst, nostrils wide and blowing, single milky blue eye rolling in his equine skull.

"Boss, it ain't natural," said one of the men, and the boss rolled his own eyes, hissing at him.

"Of course it ain't natural--it's magic," he said, narrowing his eyes at both of us--me, standing beside Satin, and Belinda, seated still in the cart.

I could hardly breathe as the men went to the back of the cart, as they began to rummage around. Belinda slipped down, mouthed at me, "What are we supposed to do?" I shrugged, shaking my head, sliding the little knife Ragla had given me down my sleeve, into my palm. Quiet as a mouse, I slid the blade against the leather of Satin's harness, cutting through the traces on this side. I ducked under his neck and did the same on the other side. Now only the dangling loops were holding the cart in place. If Satin had to leave quickly, the cart would remain, horseless. Satin, at least, would be all right.

My stomach churned. Nothing was happening at the mouth of the cart. I glanced across at Belinda. Her eyes were wide with fear, reflecting the firelight. We both looked to Merle, who knelt, completely motionless, in the center of her cage. She cocked her head, almost imperceptibly, as if to ask, "What's your plan?"

I didn't really have one. It seemed that the sort-of plan--brigands touch the mirror, curse themselves--wasn't actually *working*.

Satin blew out his breath, turned back his head. I stretched on tiptoe and peered over his shoulder. The men all stood with their heads bent over the cart bed.

I knelt down, shifted my palm so that the squiggly piece of metal I had deemed adequate to pick a lock dropped into it, and I began to work at the lock of Merle's cage.

Merle didn't move, but her eyes were wide, her chest quivering. She was panting so fast. I winked at her slowly, carefully, with my right eye, tried to smile a little. My lips were too dry. I licked them just as the lock sprang open with a gentle *click*.

Belinda's hand on my shoulder turned to claws when one of the men lifted his head, said, "Wazzat?"

Several things happened in that heartbeat. Satin snorted, kicking out with his back hooves, squarely landing them against the cart. Because of this, the cart shifted backwards, as did its heavy contents. I heard the mirror screeching across its bed of gold, saw it land squarely against the biggest brigand's abdomen, as I swung open the cage door, panicked, reaching for Merle. She gripped my hands tightly, rose, winced, and I was lifting her up and out as chaos broke loose. The men began to scream, and their screams turned high-pitched and deafening. Satin knelt down, and Belinda leaped onto his back, holding out her arms for Merle.

I boosted her up, turned to look back before I mounted myself.

The men were changing...transforming. My breath caught in my throat as their necks lengthened and their heads grew, everything turning a bright, angry gold. I scrambled up behind both Belinda and Merle, and then Satin was running, fast and surefooted in the darkness as the screams became a roar.

"I don't know what they're becoming," Belinda shouted over her shoulder, "but they sound *very angry*, Envy. What are we going to do?"

"It's dark, and this is a cursed forest. They won't find us," I muttered to her, shaking my head. But a splintering sound followed the roar, and then I heard a low *hissssssss*. My skin crawled as Satin leaped over a downed tree, racing with all of his might through a forest that had suddenly blossomed into light.

Fire.

"What's happening?" murmured Merle. Why did she look so pale? I pressed my fingers to her forehead, hissing myself. She was feverish.

"Satin, can you get us to Maria's?"

Immediately, the horse changed course.

Behind us came the creaking and thrashing of a falling tree. I tried to glance over my shoulder, but we passed over a fallen tree ourselves at that moment, and I almost fell off Satin, gripping Merle with all my might.

"If anything happens," she whispered, voice small, cracking, "I love you."

"Oh, please don't say that," I muttered, when another crash came behind us, the roar of the fire growing. What had the brigands transformed into? Monsters? Dragons? Could dragons exist? But, really, wasn't that a ludicrous question given the fact that I was gripping the waist of a blackbird girl?

What was *happening*?

Soon, Satin was crashing through the hedge and underbrush that surrounded Maria's cabin. Maria stood in the doorway, the golden cat on her shoulder, her mouth set in a very firm line.

"Merle," she whispered, as Belinda and I dropped to the ground, as I caught Merle, who tripped, leaning against me. She couldn't keep her eyes open.

"Envy," said Maria then, taking one look at the blackbird girl, then fixing me with flashing eyes. "Listen to me very closely and very carefully. The mirror... The mirror didn't do what you wanted it to do. I feel it, through the earth. Something went wrong. I think the curses combined." She looked over my shoulder, eyes narrowing. I glanced behind me, where the forest was lit up, the fire spreading. Shouldn't the snow be slowing it? I swallowed.

"Envy, *listen*," Maria hissed, taking me by the shoulders. "Merle is very sick. I have to heal her. I can't take time to reverse the curse, and if it's not reversed, Bran Wood will be destroyed. You have to reverse it."

"Me?" I laughed, but the word came out mangled, crumpled. "The curse *can't* be reversed!"

"This one *can* be. It isn't a true curse. It's a distortion, a mistake."

"How?" I wailed, rubbing at my eyes. Why was nothing ever *simple*? Merle crouched in the snow, wavering, and all I wanted to do was lift her up, put her in bed, take *care* of her.

"If you don't do this, Merle *will die*. We will all die," said Maria. "You're the only one besides me with magical training. You have to set the reversal spell."

"She never taught me reversal spells..."

"All you have to do is set it. Like any spell," she said, eyes steady. "You can set a spell, Envy."

It was too much. I looked over my shoulder at the spreading flames, the flames that licked through the ancient trees. I listened to the crash and roar of wood devoured. If I failed, there was no saving any of us. And I *would* fail. Of course I would fail.

I was common.

Common people could not do magic.

Common people...

Maria pressed a bottle into my hands, Satin bowed before me, waiting for me to mount, to go.

Belinda knelt down beside Merle, and I wavered there, truly and completely petrified.

It was Merle who broke through, Merle who lifted up her chin, who looked up at me, breathed out, skin slick with sweat and fever.

"You came for me," she said, with wonder. "You came back."

I crouched beside her, crying--I couldn't hold back the tears--and I kissed her forehead gently.

"Of course I did," I told her then. "I love you."

I rose, holding the bottle against my breast. I tucked it down and into the top of my dress, crawling up onto Satin. I took a deep breath, held on tightly to his shoulder blades, tried to focus, tried to remember everything Merle had ever taught me, but the only thing that cut through my thoughts was Merle herself--Merle, who lifted her head once more and whispered, "I love you, too."

Satin shifted and turned, fast as light, and then we were away, running through the cursed forest, Bran Wood, with a bottle warming against my heart, oddly enough, I realized, in the same place I used to hide my stolen treasures.

The smoke was suffocating. I couldn't breathe. Luckily, Satin didn't need to breathe, and he plowed through the flames as I clung to his bones, coughing, wheezing. It was like moving through the sun, I thought, feeling my fingers slip. Caught in the center of the glowing orb, I was suspended. Then Satin completed the jump, and I was bounced back to myself against the horse's rotting neck.

The men were gone, but the flame devoured everything. It licked and ate up the snow; the rotting logs, once covered with winter's blanket, were laid bare, like veins, and gobbled. The trees fell around us. The fire was moving too fast, so unlike the fires in the grates at the palace, or in the center of Envied Mansion, or even the bonfires I'd danced around, friendly fire, contained fire. This was wild, monster fire. I had never seen anything like it.

But still, would real wildfire race up a tree covered in snow so quickly? Would the wildfire eat up snow itself?

Somehow, Satin found the tower, and I dismounted--or, fell off, really--in the melee. I covered my face with the cloak, coughing so hard, I thought I might lose my lungs through my nose. I was so uncertain of what to do, and the flames arched overhead, almost taller than the tower, which stood untouched, the stone unburnable.

Satin stood beside me, shaking his head over and over. "I don't like it, Envy," he said, putting his mouth close to my ear. "This fire isn't burning like a real fire should--"

We both jumped when a nearby tree broke and shrieked as it fell, flames eating it up almost before it reached the ground.

"I think the fire is...is *alive*, sentient," said Satin then, in my ear. "I think they turned into the fire--the brigands. That was the curse, gone wrong."

I stared at him, mouth open, but then I began to cough. It didn't matter what was happening, what the villains had transformed into. If I could set the curse reversal, everything would stop.

"I have to find the mirror," I shouted to Satin. He seemed to nod, and then we inched forward, moving against the gusts of the blaze, toward where the cinders of the cart remained.

The gold was molten, it seemed, in this ridiculous living light. There, in the pile of coins and crowns and melting goblets (were they really melting? Was it a trick of my imagination?), lay the mirror, oozing with gold along its edges, frame burning.

I closed my eyes, fished the bottle up and out, stared at how tiny it was, seated in the palm of my hand.

"Envy, hurry--the fire and wind are shifting," said Satin, even as I lifted my arm, and-- as hard as I could--I hurled the tiny bottle against the mirror.

Both shattered.

"Set, set, set," I muttered, pushing with all of my might at the energy inside of me, just like Merle had instructed. I saw her, in that moment, laughing in the starlight. I breathed out, and there was a great, sizzling roar so loud I covered my ears, dropped to my knees.

Silence.

I breathed in and out, in and out, coughing through the smoke. Satin whickered at me, pushing me with his nose. "It's gone. It's all gone," he said with wonderment. "Envy, it's all gone."

I opened my eyes. It was true.

After the blaze and fire, my sight was covered in purple spots. I could hardly see. I stood, gripping onto Satin's shoulder blade, breathing, breathing. "Merle," I managed, croaking, even as I heard groans coming from around the cart. The men were there, lying on their backs, but reasonably unharmed. They began to stir as I clambered up and onto Satin, as the horse turned and raced again through the forest. Now the silent trees were sentinels, tall and still and smoking.

I clung to Satin, the last of my strength used up as we finally reached the Haglin's cottage. The stars seemed to roar through the heavens, and I fell off Satin's back, landing in a heap at his feet. I staggered upright, then to the door, which I knocked upon with a trembling hand.

Belinda opened the door, gaped at me, caught me as I fell in. I heard distant voices, heard a roaring, like a fire, but someone said, "It's all right," and I fell into blackness, content.

Merle had said it was all right.

Merle was saved.

*

The first thing: so tired. I will sleep *forever*. Forever actually does not sound like long enough. Forever and a single day. That is how long I will sleep. Sleep.

Sleep.

The second thing: *Merle*.

I opened my eyes.

She was *there*.

"She's awake!" Merle cried out, and then she was so close, and I felt her hand in mine. She gripped me tight enough to feel her heartbeat. I blinked, long and slow and lazy.

"Finally, the sleeper returns," snorted Belinda, who also appeared in my vision, though she didn't really *look* like she was joking. She actually looked so relieved that she might start crying again, and I couldn't stand to see her cry.

"Hello," I said, working my mouth up and down. I tasted as if I'd been chewing on a sweater. "Merle," I said, but she kissed me very quickly, chewing-on-sweater breath or no, then she sat back, eyes shining.

"What," she kissed me again, "did I tell you," again, "about making certain," again, "that the spell was grounded? That you didn't use your *own* energy to seal it? *What did I tell you*?" Her eyes searched mine. Her relief was almost palpable. If I'd *had* any energy, I might have blushed.

"I forgot?" I said, which seemed an acceptable answer, because she was laughing with relief, and so was Belinda, and Maria was shaking her head in the background, but she was smiling, too. The cat on her shoulder might have been smiling, also, but I'm not very good at reading cats.

"We're glad to have you among the land of the living again, dear girl," said Maria, sinking closer in my vision. "You frightened us. You're actually very powerful! Congratulations! But you use magic terribly. I should give you a quick course..."

I groaned. "I don't think I ever want to use magic again." Every part of me ached as if I'd been clobbered by Mama Leone. I tried to sit up, could not actually move my arms, so I flopped like a fish for a moment before I decided that, really, I could just lie here for a little while longer.

Belinda coughed a bit at that moment, winked, and then she and Maria were moving away from the bed, presumably to give Merle and me some alone time. Which was the least smooth, most obvious gesture I'd ever witnessed, but I wheezed and coughed and laughed, so grateful that...well. That nothing else mattered.

Merle took up my hand, pressed the palm to her cheek, stared down at me, wide-eyed. "I thought I'd never see you again," she whispered. "But you're here. You're *here*, Envy."

"I'm terribly hard to get rid of," I tried, coughing again, but she shook her head.

"You risked your life to save me. Multiple times. Envy..."

I coughed again, shifted my shoulders. The longer I lay awake, the more body parts I could move. That was a step forward, in my opinion.

"I love you," I told her, simply. "You would have done the same for me. Your dad said, 'that's how you know.' He was right. I love you--" I repeated, but she silenced me with a kiss.

"Envy," she whispered, after a very long moment. My heart thundered in my chest, and when she looked at me like that... I was already weak, but I felt myself grow weaker.

"Yes?" I managed.

"Will you marry me--" But I stopped her before she finished, laughing and wheezing, and I found I could move enough to gently gather her into my arms.

"Yes, yes, of course," I said. "Always. Forever. Yes..."

There was not enough *yes-ness* in the world to answer her question satisfactorily, so I stopped trying to use words and kissed her, instead.

Yes.

*

On the thirteenth day, Satin and I stood, shoulder to shoulder, peering down into the hole he'd come from. He sighed, long and low, and I leaned against him, still not strong enough to stand. Each day, I was getting better, growing stronger, my strength filtering back in the oddest, smallest of ways. Today, I had been able to eat a sandwich. It was the best sandwich I had ever had.

I'd made the ultimate of vows: no more magic, not ever again. Merle had not objected.

"You were wonderful," I told Satin, and hugged his head gently. He allowed me to, nosing me at the end, impatient. He was tired. He had been so good. He deserved his rest.

Maria, too, embraced him, holding his rotting head in her arms. "My most faithful of friends--thank you," she whispered into his flicking ear. He sighed and nodded, then stepped down into the hole, laying curled up like a little foal.

"Good night," he told us, even though it was morning. And he laid down his head and died.

I rubbed at my eyes furiously as Maria wept, taking up the beating red thing, so small, so fragile, from his side where it appeared, and then she held it out to me. I gripped it gingerly, felt its warmth and weight in my palm, stared down at it in silence. So small, so fragile, this thing that gave me life. It dissolved, after a long moment, shimmering into nothingness--assumedly going home beneath my breast--and there in Maria's fingers lay the green apple.

We stood for a long time, feeling the cold of the winter wrap us up and close. My blackbird girl stood on my shoulder, twisting her head this way and that. She let out a *caw*, flying up and over the shallow grave.

"I miss him so much already," Maria said, drawing her cloak closer about herself. "Sometimes, it is very lonely here. He was the best of friends." The tears traced down her cheeks without shame. Belinda and I exchanged a glance.

"I...I can't really speak for Ragla. But he seemed very fond of you. And Night Village...it probably has no witch," I told her. Maria looked up, her face a question.

As if in answer, Merle fluttered over again, hopping down and in front of the Haglin, bobbing her head fiercely.

So that was that.

*

We walked to the Blackbird Kingdom like any true supplicants--on our own two feet. After crisscrossing Bran Wood on the back of a rotting horse, this seemed an awfully slow way to travel.

It had snowed, the white blanket of winter making soft curves of the downed trees, those gobbled up and devoured by the unnatural flames of a curse gone wrong. The parts of the forest that had been destroyed looked almost beautiful with those equalizing drifts. And, anyway, Maria informed us, ashes made the soil rich. New trees would spring up where the old had stood. And Bran Wood would rebuild itself.

Merle and I walked arm and arm in the cold winter sunshine. Belinda and Maria strolled beside us, and long distant behind Maria stretched a very long line of very unhappy and cold cats. She lured them on with the promises of milk and warm hearths in Night Village. I think they only half-believed her.

We made plans, and we made promises, and as the sun dipped down in the heavens, kissing the earth with gold, we came upon Night Village and the Nightmare Gate. John stood at the entrance, waving a single white wing back and forth, grin wide and jubilant.

I chanced a glance at Merle, her face open, joyful. Her love...mine.

Here's what I knew, just then, knew like tricks and thievery, like common truths and luck made and found: a heart can be stolen or given freely. Sometimes both, at the same time.

The almost-Blackbird Queen and her bride went home.

The End

About the Author

Elora Bishop is a queer lady author. You will often find her wearing soft skirts, curled up in a sunny window (much like a cat), Austen in hand, cup of tea (two cream, one sugar) nearby, always piping hot. She is bewitched by all beautiful things–but, most of all, by her beloved partner.

Elora writes magical lesbian love stories, and releases new ones quite regularly. You can find out about her upcoming novels or her previous works at http://elorabishop.wordpress.com and at http://www.twitter.com/elorabishop

She adores correspondences and loves hearing from her fans and friends--you can pen her an email at elorabish@gmail.com

22292579R00113

Made in the USA
Lexington, KY
24 April 2013